A car picks us up at noon. The chauffeur is completely silent . . .

'Good morning my man,' says Kate jovially after about five minutes . . .

'Where are we going?'

'I'm not allowed to say, miss.' . . .

'That is the end of another sparkling conversation, Kate.'

'I once knew a chauffeur.'

'Marvellous lovers, they say, like milkmen.'

'Fabulous. The best.'

Poker-face never even looks in the mirror, which is a pity for him, because Kate is having a lot of trouble with her new tights and is trying to take them off as we go. Although it is a big car she is making very heavy weather of it. Her skirt is practically over her head. Finally she opens a window and chucks them out, practically blinding a boy on a bicycle.

'You won't need those in Mexico.' . . .

'I shouldn't think we'll need clothes at all.'

Penny Sutton

The Jumbo Jet Girls

Futura Publications Limited

A Futura Book

First published in Great Britain in 1974
by Futura Publications Limited

ISBN 0 8600 7134 0

Printed in Great Britain by
Cox & Wyman Ltd
London, Reading and Fakenham

Futura Publications Limited
49 Poland Street, London W1A 2LG

CHAPTER 1

When my flying friend Kate Goodbody and I got back from our adventures in Australia, we didn't see each other for a while. It wasn't that we weren't still friends. It was just that we had seen so much shattered, so many hopes crushed. Also, if I'm honest, which I try to be, I began to behave in a way that deep down was not me. I had lots of casual affairs, really as a way to forget Ross.* So many that I didn't want Kate to know. As it turns out, Kate felt the same about seeing me, and for the same reasons. We were jaded and a little saddened. Sex is a comfort at times like this, though about as meaningful as a cup of Ovaltine at bedtime. Anyway all these cups of Ovaltine came and went. (Came and came, Kate said later.)

One evening I went to a party, one of those parties where someone distinctly almost remembers a recipe for punch their uncle used to make in India. Lots of white wine, the dregs of numerous liqueur bottles, bits of massacred fruit and a prayer. Animal passions were beginning to rise like a hot fog (to be followed by everyone's dinner) when suddenly I saw Richard.

'Hi,' he said, 'I'm Richard.'

'I'm sure you are.' Inwardly I was thinking here we go again, but not too reluctantly. He was a little long-haired and pansy-looking for my normal tastes, but when he smiled it was a strong, confident face.

'What do you do?'

'Nothing at the moment. What about you?'

'Anything I can lay my hands on.'

As you can see, the conversation was skipping along merrily. But he spoke with a sort of softness and friendliness that made me think, although they were so different in age, of Ross.

'I'm a photographer, as it happens. Not in the David Bailey class just yet, but I'm getting there.'

*See *The Stewardesses Down Under* for details of Ross, and Penny and Kate's adventure with Outback Airlines.

Now Kate and I had once done some modelling before becoming stewardesses, so I knew all about photographers. But there was no invitation to come and see the studio. Or to do a few tests, as they call them; really tests to see how much they can get off. No. He just chatted me up casually in his nice soft Scots accent. I'm a mug for the cool, confident approach. So I was surprised and a little hurt when he drifted off, saying he would call the next day.

'Hello, gorgeous,' said a well-boozed young pilot I once flew with. He was in that happy state you get to after six glasses of punch. Fixed, frozen smile. Face slightly flushed.

'You're looking lovely,' he said, staring at a point about a foot below my face. I was wearing a dress, of which daddy would not have approved, which showed the remains of my Australian tan to best advantage, and also one of my best features. I'm not actually enormous, like Kate, but I can stand up with the best of them, if you know what I mean.

'I'm going on somewhere exciting. Do you want to come?'

'What do you call exciting?' Errol is a notorious exaggerator.

'It's a party given by one of those Arab Airlines.'

'I don't go for the Latin type much,' I said tactfully. But I was thinking of the lunatic hijacker, Hamid, him of the staring wild eyes and my voice didn't carry much conviction. Although, basically I prefer the Anglo-Saxon type, unlike Kate, sometimes a girl needs a little gush and romance. Foreigners are so much better at it than our home-grown lads. So, to cut a long story short, I went.

It was a huge house in Belgravia. The sort of place where the street is very quiet and sedate, but inside you would imagine all sorts of goings-on. And you wouldn't be far wrong. I have never seen anything like it. Servants in Bedouin robes everywhere. A mixture of very smooth Lebanese businessmen in well-cut suits, preceded by an early warning of after-shave, oil tycoons and young girls, obviously mostly stewardesses. Beside a huge buffet, groaning with good things, were a few musicians playing strange, hypnotic Arab music, like the background for a Kasbah movie. Victor Mature expected on the next camel train. And above all the reek of money. The servants all carried jewelled daggers, and an enormous, elderly Arab gentleman sat in state in a huge carved chair. All inlaid ivory and winking stones, like a prop from East Cheam Amateur Dramatic Society's production of *The Pirates of Penzance*.

I loved it. The rich and the powerful, for all the disappointments I have had, still fascinate me.

Errol, the pilot, was steering me with a hand cunningly placed so as to be interpreted by the pure-minded as on the small of my back, towards a group of clean-cut young drunks. Obviously pilots and stewardesses. Laughing a lot, and swopping stories about other less accomplished airlines. Airlines whose stewardesses are all nymphomaniacs, whose pilots' only training is in World War One bi-planes, whose food is American Aid Surplus and so on, and on. There is a lot of glamour to flying, but really I sometimes wish crews would stop talking shop.

So I slipped away. By now the wretched Errol had his hand on somebody's shoulder, just touching the top of one boob. Old Errol really should give up the fluttering hands, it's such a DOM trick. If you want to touch, touch like a dirty young man I say, openly. Anyway, I walked up a curved staircase to the first floor, looking for a likely place to fix my hair and inspect my face before sallying forth amongst the money. The first door I opened was a bedroom of some sort. But the floor was strewn with carpets, cushions and mattresses together, all low and sexy, like a mosque gone depraved. A small door led to a bathroom, where I started to do something with my hair. Since I got back from Australia, I hadn't been able to get Laurent at Vital Balloon's to do it for me every week. Oh, how I need a job I was thinking, just so I could buy back Laurent's undying care and attention. What an artist that lad is, and so sexy with his tight carefully faded jeans and silk shirts, and what a pity he's a bit ginger beer, too.

As my mind is drifting idly along in this fashion, I hear sounds of action in the next room. Now I am in something of a dilemma, because the sounds, quite distinct, suggest that what's going on is not blind man's buff, though something is going to happen the way things are hotting up.

'Come to me. Come to me my darrrrling, my little turrrtle dove.' You know the way Arabs roll the r's, like King Hussein.

Scuffle, scuffle.

'Come to me. Let me take you in my arrms.'

'You talked me into it, you desert lover, you,' says the other voice clearly. It's Kate! Kate Goodbody, putting it into practice.

'I must have you now. Mount my proud stallion.' Obviously something of a poet.

'Just a moment, Excellency,' says Kate. 'I won't be a moment.' And she comes into the bathroom and shuts the door.

'Mount my proud stallion,' say I.

Kate and I become nearly hysterical as we try to laugh in whispers.

'For Chrissake, Penny, I have got to get out of here.' She is mostly out of her dress already. She starts to button up and tuck herself in. This is quite a job, because she is wearing a black bra that Twiggy would find constricting.

'I'll explain later, but I've got to get out of here without offending the old boy.'

From the next room comes a noise, which even to those untutored in Berber, sounds impatient. If not angry.

'I know,' say I, looking into the medicine cabinet, 'let's knock him out with some pills.'

'Penny, you're still reading *Crystal* despite my warnings. By the time you've knocked the old boy out he'll have crushed me to death. He weighs twenty stone.'

'Don't let it get on top of you.' Even the humour is getting a little forced, I note.

'I'll have to go back in. I was hoping I could get out through here. Try and create a diversion. Please,' she begs.

The noises from the next room sound menacing. Poor Kate goes in to meet her fate, with a wry smile.

'My little dove, come to me.' All that drivel starts again. I peek through the door. Kate is undressing slowly, with occasional desperate looks towards the bathroom. Fortunately there are a lot of buttons on that particular dress. Lying propped up on a pile of cushions is the large, important old gentleman from downstairs. His robes are in a state of disarray.

Suddenly I have a brainwave. I pull all the loo paper out of the holder, put it in the bath, which, of necessity, is enormous, with a towel for good measure and light the lot. It

8

takes a few moments to get going but soon it begins to billow smoke gratifyingly. As it fills the bathroom I fling open the door and rush into the room screaming *'Fire! Fire!'* A huge cloud of smoke follows me. That makes my performance quite believable, though I pose no immediate threat to Maggie Smith. Kate, I notice, is down to her briefs, and never were briefs briefer. The Excellency is wearing a pair of jockey shorts, but at least three jockeys Lester Piggott's size could get lost in them. He is also wearing socks and suspenders and his burnouse, which makes him look like a whale dressing up as Lawrence of Arabia.

'Hurry, Excellency, Hurry,' says Kate.

The old fellow misunderstands her intentions and starts to peel off his enormous jockey shorts. It's a bit like the marquee coming down after a barmitzvah.

'No, no,' says Kate, 'there's a fire, a conflagration. Quick.'

I am still running about shouting 'Fire!' This may be a rather one-paced performance, but it gives Kate time to pull on her dress. The door bursts open and two huge black servants race in. As they begin to lever the old boy to his feet, which is going to be difficult without a block and tackle, Kate and I make our exit. Kate is bouncing a bit as we run. Many other people are rushing the other way to find out what's going on. I just hope the fire hasn't got out of hand. In an alcove Kate sets to work on her buttons, for the fourth time in a few minutes, and we make our way, as sedately as possible to the front door.

Errol intercepts us. He has with him a really fabulously good-looking guy.

'This is Skippy Rogers from Quantas,' says Errol, trying to bask in his reflected glory. 'We wondered if you'd like to get to know us better.'

Errol has his hands round my waist and is feeling the top of my thighs. Skippy is staring transfixed at Kate, who is looking a little the worse for wear. Her dress was never made to be worn without a bra, and it's only irregularly buttoned.

We both know we had better get out, but the offer is tempting.

'Some other time, Skippy.'

'Any time, Skippy, but not tonight,' adds Kate pointedly.

We hear Skippy muttering to Errol as we go, something like 'Bloody Pommie Sheilas are all teasers. Did you see the set on the scruffy one. Like two bloody great . . .' We never hear what.

'Oh my little dove, mount my stallion,' I say to Kate as I wave ineffectually at a taxi.

'No, no,' she says, 'come with me.'

Round the back in a mews she lets me into a fabulous white Dino Ferrari.

'Fell off the back of a lorry, did it?'

'Old Prince Rashmid gave it to me.'

'Gave it to you? Do you know how much these things cost?'

'No, do you?'

'A lot,' I say lamely, because I have no idea.

'He makes twelve million dollars a week.' From this I guess he's either in the property business or in oil, but seeing he's an Arab I deduce it's the latter. Kate is searching for an appropriate gear. The dials, which are numerous, are flashing and winking like a demented pinball machine, and suddenly off we go. This surprises Kate even more than me and we deal a glancing blow to a large Rolls before we hit Belgrave Square.

CHAPTER 2

The telephone rings in the depths of a deep, deep sleep the next morning. A Scots voice says:

'Hello, it's Richard.'

Despite everything, I am instantly wide awake. Richard of the soft, sexy voice, and soft sexy smile.

'Do you want to come round and do some pictures?'

'What sort?'

'Oh figure, nudies. You know the sort of thing.' I do indeed. But somehow he has disarmed me by being so open about it.

'Are you going to pay me?'

'May do.'

Again I am disarmed. Still, life has been a bit dull since we got back and I do need something to keep me from vegetating.

'OK,' I say. 'Can I bring my friend Kate along?'

'Sure, we'll have a look at her.'

'OK. What time?'

As he's about to ring off he says:

'By the way, bring your uniforms along. Don't worry, if we use them in any of the shots, we'll take the insignia off. 'Bye.' Well I know the airline we had worked for in Britain before going to Australia didn't appreciate the publicity I'd given them free and for nothing, so it seemed sensible. But how did he knew we were stewardesses? Still waters run deep, with that Richard. So I ring Kate:

'Morning, my little turtle dove.'

'Oh God,' she says, 'what a night.'

'No eunuchs been after you to take you away yet.'

'Not yet, but they will.'

'Well they are cut out for the job, aren't they?' This is a very old joke indeed, but not bad first thing in the morning. I tell her about Richard. She guesses there's more than just a professional interest, but, loyal friend, she offers to pick me up in her Ferrari, white with black dents, very pretty, in two hours.

Three hours later she appears. Despite looking a bit like a Dalmatian, the Dino still goes very fast. This must be very gratifying for the makers, because Kate tells me it's only five days old. We shoot into the Cromwell Road with such speed that the traffic parts like the Red Sea. Even taxi-drivers know when they're beaten. (They also know their Old Testament.) Kate tells me all about Prince Rashid. It's not a very edifying tale at all. In fact it's somewhat sordid. It turns out the Ferrari is given on the clear understanding that services will be rendered, and only my timely intervention stopped the whole dodgy business from reaching its inevitable climax, if you'll excuse the pun.

'As you can see, I was sailing a bit close to the wind.'

'More like already capsized.'

'They practically carried me into the old boy's room last night. Thank God you were there. Oh it is good to see you again.'

She gives me a big hug and we are so overcome by our happy reunion, that I fail to warn Kate of a pedestrian crossing.

'Don't worry, dear, they're not to stop accidents, only to localize them,' I sympathize with her after an irate mother has added yet another dent with her umbrella. As Kate points out, it's a much more complex car to drive than our old A40 which had only two serviceable gears. Kate believes this has six, though she's not sure yet. However many gears it's got, it certainly makes you feel important. Taxi-drivers, truck drivers even boys on mopeds, stare in at us. They wave, they hoot, they smile ingratiatingly. Too late we have discovered that you can't really ride about lying back as though you were at the dentists, in a short skirt, which both of us are wearing as it's a lovely spring day.

'Lie back and enjoy it,' I advise Kate. She has been anyway, long since.

'I am,' she says, 'I remembered my knickers this morning.'

In fact, it turns out, so have I, but she gives me a nasty turn for a moment. We begin to enjoy it. I think most women are exhibitionists somewhere in their make-up. Lovely day, beautiful car, which Kate is vaguely getting the hang of, and all these admiring men. I yawn and stretch suggestively as a lorry driver practically puts his neck out of joint staring down at us.

'For Chrissake, Penny, you'll get us arrested, there's not a lot of that T-shirt as it is.' But as she says it she blows a kiss to a gentleman in a large Jag. He is dying to smile back, but his wife appears to be applying pressure to some part of his anatomy, and he manages only a half-throttled cough.

Yes, the sap is rising. We have shaken off that boredom and depression which hit us as we landed at Heathrow. Suddenly London looks summery, bright and full of possibilities again. Kate nearly ruins these prospects by getting entangled with a group of horse-riders as we cross Hyde Park. None of them fall off, to my disappointment, and we're soon in Mayfair.

Richard's studio is in a mews. He's not there, but a rather tight-lipped girl gives us a bottle of white wine and two glasses and says to have a look round, like he'll be back soon. Two huge speakers are banging out Carly Simon. The studio is on the ground floor, with a little dressing-room and reception. This is furnished with large soft, leather sofas and a fleecy white rug. Up a little spiral staircase is a gallery which is really just a big, big bed, smothered with a fur.

Kate gives me a funny look.

'Lives above the shop, you see.'

After half an hour, we're getting a bit tipsy. Still no Richard. But it's very pleasant, what with the music and the wine. We decide that perhaps modelling is the life for us. As Kate says, while you've got it, you might as well flaunt it. Modesty has never been Kate's hang-up. We're quite giggly by now, because it's about one o'clock, and a light breakfast of Riesling is not our normal routine. Though I feel I could get used to it.

Richard and a very long-haired boy appear. Richard introduces him as his assistant, Jem. Poor Jem, it appears, has to do the hard work, because Richard dispatches him to get the props and the set, as he calls them.

Kate is obviously impressed by Richard. A bit too obviously, I think cattily. The other girl, his secretary is dispatched, sulkily, for some smoked salmon sandwiches, while he opens a bottle of vintage champagne with as much interest as though it were Lucozade. I am afraid this impresses me even more. I know this is a weakness in my character, but I must be honest about it. He is wearing a T-shirt and a pair of beautiful French jeans. The French have a way of taking sloppy clothes and making them look terrific, and expensive. I notice that his legs are long and slim, though obviously muscular. This is good because I don't really go for the skinny, weedy type.

'Well, this is your friend, is it?'

'Yes. How did you know we were stewardesses?' I ask, changing the subject as fast as possible.

'I have my sources,' he says, smiling.

The second bottle of champagne and the smoked salmon sandwiches arrive simultaneously. Still no mention of what he wants us to do but we're not complaining.

'It must be very interesting being a photographer,' says Kate in a voice that would make Jayne Mansfield blush.

'Actually, it's a bit of a pain. It's not really very creative. Anybody can take pictures. I'm trying to become a director.'

He lights a cigarette. The smell is so strong I think it's Turkish tobacco, but Kate gives me a little nudge before I can say anything. Pot! At this time of day. Well, I've had pot before, and it's had no effect. I've never been able to see the point really, so when Richard hands it to me I take it as casually as I can and inhale like a good 'un, before handing it on to Kate. She does likewise trying to look as though she does it every day.

'Lebanese gold,' says Richard shortly.

'Oh yes?' says Kate, looking around expectantly. This is probably because of her recent experience with Arabs; she's become something of an expert.

'The grass. It's the best you can score.'

I nod wisely. In fact I feel as though my head is about to take off. I feel fantastic. Just like being tipsy, but without the pain. As a matter of truth, I am already tipsy as well. Richard turns the music up and we all sink back into the cushions and stare at the ceiling philosophically.

Kate gets up and begins to dance by herself. It seems quite a natural thing to do under the circumstances. Richard puts an arm around me and we have another deep draw. We watch Kate undulating sensuously; that's something else she's learned from those Arabs, by the looks of it, and then Richard gives me a deep, friendly kiss. As his mouth opens I wrap my arms around him, and my tongue and his meet and

14

caress each other. I feel deeply moved by the kiss, like one of those kisses you have as a twelve year-old behind the bicycle shed. But Richard just smiles distantly.

He gets up and says:

'Look, could you get into your airline drag, I feel like doing some pictures. Come through when you're ready.'

In something of a dream, Kate and I undress.

'Naughty,' she says affectionately.

I am wearing a very brief pair of black panties and three-quarter bra.

'Now, Kate, you know me well enough not to jump to conclusions.'

But she has, and she's right. Girls don't just put on their best underwear in case they get knocked over in traffic as my mother used to say.

As we are about half ready, a make-up man comes through and gives us a withering look.

'My dear, amateurs.'

He's never going to play rugby for Llanelli, but he's a terrific make-up artist. By the time he's finished with us, we look, quite honestly, sensational. Kate flutters her eyelashes, and we giggle. It takes us a long time to finish getting dressed – we seem to be all thumbs. But we do laugh a lot, even more than is usual with Kate, who's one of the best laughs I know. Kate has her hair pulled up under her hat, in the prescribed manner. Her skirt seems a bit shorter than I remembered her on duty in it. This, it turns out, is because she took it up a few inches this morning. She is trying to look 'Welcome aboardish', but she can't quite get it together.

We go through to the studio, and I am amazed. Little Jem sure has been busy – Jem and an army of carpenters. They've reconstructed three rows of seats from a Jumbo and made a very plausible cockpit. Richard is supervising the lighting. Over the other side of the studio is a beautiful room set, a luxurious bedroom/living-room, all fur and chrome and glass.

'All right, let's do some fairly straightforward stuff before the boys get here,' says Richard.

'Right you are, Captain,' says Kate idiotically, but we both laugh as though she were Frankie Howerd.

Taking pictures is pretty routine really. Lots of fiddling about. Richard makes us reach up for cupboards, pour drinks, hand out trays. It all looks like an ad for a package tour of the Isle of Man. Still he does seem to be getting the camera in some pretty fancy positions. Half an hour passes quite merrily in this fashion. We seem to drink at least another bottle of champagne on the way. I wish Richard would stop squinting into that viewfinder for a minute. It's obvious to me that we are just props, to use one of his favourite words, but I am feeling so warm and happy that I could forgive him anything. Trouble is, he doesn't stay still for a moment of forgiveness.

Two absolutely divine men appear, dressed for all the world like airline pilots. But they are much too dishy for that. Richard introduces them.

'This is Fred and this is Chris.'

They don't look a bit like a Fred or a Chris to me. They have such expensive suntans and that glossy, Martini look about them. More like a Justin or a Wayne, I would say. Still, they're not stuck up about being famous, as they obviously are. They drop names of directors, locations and well-known models without any obvious intention to impress, which impresses me of course.

Richard says, 'Look, I'll be about half an hour getting some more gear, so get to know each other and we'll do a few more shots when we get back.'

'Look, boys, we're well on the way, so why don't you catch up,' says Kate.

The gorgeous Fred takes me by the arm and we sit ourselves comfortably in the first-class seats at the front of one set. Fred is of that indeterminable age that some women find exciting, me included. All male models seem to be thirty-four for all time, experienced enough in the ways of the world without being passé. While I am thinking these thoughts, Fred casually slips his arm around me and fills my glass. I really am in a pretty bad state, but as his hand slips inside my blouse, I look around nervously. The studio is empty, though I can hear Kate and Chris over at the other side where the room set is. There's a loud pop of a champagne cork going off and a few laughs. The pot has made me feel so sensuous, it's unbelievable. A warm glow from Fred's hand, which is now inside my bra, spreads down to my legs. We kiss. Me and this unknown divine Fred. I am filled with an almost unbearable wave of affection for him. He opens my blouse right down to the bottom and caresses my breasts. He's obviously been in a plane, too, because he needs no help from me to raise the armrest between the seats and stretch out on his back. I have only known this man for ten minutes when I find myself undoing his zipper. But it all seems quite natural. Even if he is an international gigolo, his response to my hand is pleasing.

He has my tights off and my skirt pulled up, as I slip a leg between his. We kiss again as his hands caress me under my panties. I am so ready for him, I feel almost embarrassed. As I begin to straddle him, he says,

'No, let's go into the cockpit.'

He's right because the cockpit set is at least three-quarters enclosed and the open end faces the wall of the studio. The truth is, the way I feel fabulous Fred could suggest Trafalgar Square, and I'd go. This is no time to digress, but the strong confident approach which Fred must have invented, is a winner with me. He sits in the captain's seat and I take off my panties. The bizarreness of the whole scene just makes it more exciting for me. I have once done this before, my initiation to the Mile High Club, so I am no slouch at lowering myself on to his lap. It's an outsize seat for a cockpit really but that's artistic licence, I think happily as he slides into me. Oh God! My whole body seems to be involved, I want to be kissed and caressed all over, every inch of me is keyed up to bursting. Fred obliges faithfully. His face has a look of ecstasy on it as he begins to kiss my breasts. Wave on wave of feeling floods through me; I come once, twice, three times, before he does. As I kiss him, I notice that because of the hot lights we're both rather damp. Fred gets the champagne out, as I slump in the seat next to him, and douses my front. I am practically unconscious.

Richard, whom I've forgotten, chooses this moment to reappear. I am terribly embarrassed because you don't have to be Chief Ironside to guess what we've been doing. Fred doesn't say a thing – just smiles smugly.

Richard, mercifully, also smiles.

'I see, OK, we'll call it a day. Your friend Kate looks as though she needs a rest too. See you tomorrow.'

And that was the beginning and the end of our modelling career.

CHAPTER 3

The next day Richard does not ring. Nor do Fred and Chris. Which is a pity because Kate and I agree, though struck down by monumental hangovers, that they are the most beautiful pair of men that we have ever met. At least I have the comfort of knowing that Kate met a similar fate to mine, though in her case in the comfort of a big bed.

'That pot and champagne made me forget I had only known Chris a few minutes,' she says by the way of a justification.

'He can't be called Fred, really, can he?'

'I don't know. The whole business is a bit strange in the cold light of day, if you ask me.'

I have had the same rather depressing feeling myself all morning.

'Let's give him a ring,' say I.

So I ring Richard's studio.

'Hello, can I speak to Richard please.'

'Who is that?'

'It's Penny Sutton.'

'Oh yes,' says the tight-lipped lady, 'Before he left Richard said that if you rang to say he would call when he gets back from Bermuda next week.'

As I can hear Richard talking to someone in the background, I say, 'Tell little Dickie not to forget to take his bucket and spade,' and slam down the phone. A bit of pique, that gets me nowhere.

'Oh well,' says Kate, 'put it down to experience.'

Experience is all very well, but it does not pay the bills. We decide to sell Kate's car. Actually Kate is unbelievably generous about this because I haven't done a thing to earn a share. But then nor did she, as she points out, thanks to me. We call a garage in the West End who specialize in expensive sports cars.

'Certainly, madam, we'll send one of our chaps round tomorrow morning to have a look at it. Two weeks old, I see. Well the list price is about £6,500 for this sort of model:

though of course it's a rather specialized market, so we may not be able to offer you the full amount, you understand.'

His patter would make Doctor Kildare sound insincere.

'Six thousand five hundred pounds?'

'Less a few hundred for all the dents.'

'Well, say six thousand. We could have a Mini each and go on a fantastic holiday for about three years.'

The mind boggles at the prospect of such wealth. It boggles away all night, but the next morning we are in for a bit of a disappointment. The salesman from the car company, after tut-tutting about the dents, offers us £5,800. We agree with a show of reluctance. Unfortunately he wants to have the log-book.

I look at Kate. I know it was too good to be true in my heart of hearts. We look in the glove compartment. Kate doesn't actually know what a log-book is, but she senses its importance, because the salesman is looking her sternly in the face for the first time since he arrived. Prior to that, his eyes seemed to be magnetized by her admittedly, magnificent boobs. I try the last throw of the dice. I take his hand and hold it to my chest.

'Surely you can help us. We do own it you know – it was given to us.' I look deep into his eyes.

'Look,' he says, 'to sell a car in this country you need proof of ownership. It's none of my business, but there are people,' he doesn't actually wink but it's an upper class version of same, 'who are not as scrupulous as we.'

'Tell me more,' I say squeezing his hand, softly.

'Well, I'll arrange for someone, to get in touch with you, off the record of course.'

His Hector Powe suit seems to be under pressure at various points. I lean forward and give him a little kiss.

'And we'll be terribly grateful,' says Kate, licking her lips to indicate a whole world of promise.

After he's gone I say,

'You're turning into a tart.'

'What about you?'

'Well, he'll never come back to collect. Anyway he's got to go home to Croydon on the 5.27.'

'I wouldn't be too sure.'

All we're sure of is that we haven't got a bean and that we need a job desperately. Our verdict on modelling: fun but not financially secure. In the back of my mind I am still hoping Richard is going to come good though. But flying is really our game.

That evening the phone rings.

'Ullo.'

'Hello, with whom am I speaking,' says Kate rather posh.

'Never mind, dear. I hear you want to sell a car.'

'A Ferrari.'

'Sure, I know all about it. Old crock fell off of a lorry, on nose, more bleeding dents than 'Enry Cooper. Your friend told me. That's not all he told me, neither.'

'It's only a few days old.'

'Well, look here, I'll give you twelve hundred, no, call that twelve hundred and fifty nicker, I'm in a generous mood, the wife's going on holiday soon.'

'But it's worth five times that amount.'

'You don't say. Not to me it ain't. Do you want it? I'm a very busy man.' He begins to hum.

'OK,' says Kate.

'Good man. Leave it outside this evening. No keys. Frow them away, into the Thames if you like. I'll send the money round soon.'

'Look, we own this car, it's not illegal you know,' says Kate, her chest heaving.

'Did I say it was illegal. Did anybody hear me say it was illegal. I'm in the motor trade, pure and simple, nothing dodgy for me.' His voice registers so much pain, I can see him mopping his anguished brow, a small man trying to turn an honest penny for his wife and kids.

A boy in leathers and a helmet delivers a brown paper parcel two hours later. He says nothing, picks his nose as we sign the slip, and hops on to his motorcycle. It's money. Twelve hundred and fifty pounds in fivers.

'It's not illegal is it, really, deep down, I mean?' I ask Kate, who is staring at it all transfixed as she lays it out in bundles. We're rich. Rich.

The next few days are a dream. I buy half of Harrods, including a parrot from a dishy man in the zoo. He could have sold me an aardvark for all I cared. The parrot begins to look very sick indeed when it sees my flat; the poor thing is obviously used to a better class of lodging altogether. Kate gives it some gin to cheer it up, but it proves conclusively that alcohol is a depressant by lying moodily on its back in the bottom of the cage.

We have a nasty turn when the car salesman turns up unexpectedly. We decide to play it very innocent. He is wearing a pair of cavalry twill trousers and a polo-neck sweater, in an attempt to look 'with-it' as he calls it. Pity about the brown brogues underneath.

'Would you like some tea?' I ask. 'Miss Goodbody and I were just about to commence to have some.'

Miss Goodbody enters into the spirit of the thing.

'How many children do you have? We adore children, don't we, Penelope? One lump or two?'

Actually, I'm beginning to feel a little sorry for him, as he now looks as comfortable as a pork chop in a synagogue. He sips his tea with little finger nicely crooked in the air, as though expecting a butterfly to land on it at any moment. Kate shows no mercy. She asks him brightly about his wife, home, children, pension prospects and so on without giving him a chance to suggest that he is really a carefree bachelor with a pad (borrowed) near the Angel tube station where he's going to take us in his Lamborghini (borrowed from the office) after dinner at a little Trat he knows (cheap), while his wife thinks he's at a car dealers convention in Newport Pagnell.

'Well I must be off,' he says as breezily as he can manage.

'Oh no, do stay,' says Kate. 'Penny and I have always wanted to know all about East Croydon. Is it a pretty place, well served by public transport, and dotted with nice little parks, as one hears tell?'

This would be a perfectly good place to end our association with Phillip as he's called. But the devil in me decides to make his evening memorable at least.

'Just you two go on talking among yourselves,' I say, 'I've got to get ready to go to a meeting of the Young Fabians, but don't mind me.'

My flat, as the landlord calls it with some degree of exaggeration, is really only one large room with a kitchen and bathroom. The bed is half partitioned off by a low chest of drawers, which would probably have done nicely as orange crates if they weren't so full of worm. I slip off my jeans and smock behind this and put on a dressing-gown.

'Do help yourself to a sherry, Phillip,' say I leaning forward to indicate a bottle of British Rich Tawny which the landlord obviously left behind as a deterrent to cockroaches.

Poor Phillip. He can't help noticing that my dressing-gown is a little loose above the waist. And not too snug below either.

'I'm just going to have a bath, but I won't be long.'

As I go into the bathroom I let the dressing-gown fall and half shut the door. In a mirror Phillip can just about see in the door. The gas heater begins its ritual groanings, a few drops of water emerge and lots of steam, and I stand in front of the bath expectantly wearing only a pair of panties. As I peel these off I turn round and see for a moment Phillip's tortured face in the mirror before steam envelops me. Kate is still talking earnestly about the commuting problems on the Southern Region.

I empty about a quart of new expensive, bath oil into the bath and sink into the green, lovely water. I have put so much bath oil in it that I feel like a slimy gila monster. But it is very sensuous all the same.

'Kate, would you be so kind as to give me another cup of tea in here?'

'Phillip, do take Penelope a cup of tea.'

Phillip appears through the steam. He begins to wipe his glasses.

'Over here. Just put it down there. Oh gosh, you seem to have dropped your glasses. Never mind, I'll find them for you.'

Phillip's trousers, what I can see of them begin to wilt in the steam. I fish his glasses out of the murky waters and hand them back to him. He shows no inclination to leave, and is staring at the high-water mark which is about a centimetre above my nipples.

'Katherine, I think Phillip wants another cup of tea.'

'Here we are, Phillip, come on out. Penelope must not be late for the young Fabians. Most punctual people, your young Fabians.'

Eventually I dry myself, and come back into the room. I emerge from behind the chest of drawers wearing a black, three-quarter bra and a new pair of jeans.

'Kate, what shall I wear with these new jeans?'

'I think a blue denim shirt would be nice. What do you think, Philip. You obviously have lots of dress sense.'

I try it on. Then a very tight sweater. Then we decide I would look more Fabian in a full-length peasant skirt with a cheesecloth blouse, no bra, more swinging.

'What do you think, Phillip?' asks Kate innocently.

'Yes.'

'Yes, what?'

'Yes she would.'

And he is right. I look terrific. I almost feel like becoming a young Fabian right away.

'Well, Phillip, when I get back from the Nye Bevan Memorial Hall in Cricklewood, perhaps we can have another cup of tea and a chat.'

Phillip's interest in politics is obviously slight, because he seems to want to go now. He gets up and says firmly:

'No, no, I've had enough tea. Before I go I would just like to leave you with a present.' And off he goes, leaving a magazine on the table. 'Enjoy the young Fabians.'

Do I detect a sneer, a sneer of contempt for a fine institution? I do.

'Well, you've solved your job problem. You could always get a job in Soho,' says Kate.

'We could open the first topless tea-shop.'

'Wonder what he left this for. I thought he looked a bit kinky.'

It's a man's magazine, which I look through casually. Most of the girls are not nearly as pretty or nearly as well-built as Kate or me. Suddenly my heart stops. Two of the girls are Kate and me! In uniform (well, half in) with Fred and Chris. My God. It all falls into place. The feature is called *Sex in the Sky. Fly Girls Tell All.* And there we are! The only mercy is that they have used false names. Richard. The little Scots bastard.

After a while we begin to giggle hysterically.

'In the cockpit. You never told me.'

'What about you. Rolling about on that big bed.'

There are about ten full colour shots of us, accompanied by a story that is, mercifully, totally false.

'Really, I think you look quite fetching in the cockpit.' I

23

don't like the way she says 'cockpit' at all. She is looking at a picture of Fred with his hands inside my blouse and my skirt practically under my chin.

'Funny how you never see the men exposed, isn't it?'

'Well, they were obviously in on the secret.'

'Bastards.'

Kate is particularly embarrassed by a shot of her sitting astride Chris with her hat still on her head.

'Mount my proud stallion,' I say, cruelly.

'Bloody shut up. Look at you, in the first-class seats too.' It hurts. Richard has captured my expression as my hands undo Fred's zipper. I could practically cry.

But crying isn't going to help us. What we need is plastic surgery and a one-way trip to Brazil or preferably somewhere even more remote.

CHAPTER 4

Help comes from an unexpected quarter. Richard. He rings up quite casually the next morning, or more like early afternoon. Kate and I can't bear to get out of bed. We expect people to throw rotten fruit and laugh at us. Richard is so cool, I manage only one little dig.

'Had a lovely time in Bermuda?'

'Couldn't do the job,' he says, 'too busy. Old Parks had to do it.'

'Poor old Parks,' I say sympathetically.

Kate shouts at the telephone, something about what she would do to him if he ever appeared in his kilt in her part of town.

'Look,' says Richard. 'I've made you girls famous. You might as well learn to live with it. After all there's nothing else you can do.'

This is, of course, true but bloody infuriating all the same.

'Look' (I wish he would stop saying 'look', every time a dagger between the ribs follows), 'I've got someone who wants to meet you.'

'Terrific. Where are you going to hide with the camera this time. Under the bed?' I am struggling a bit to keep on terms, as they say in the racing world.

'Look, it's Hiram Firefly. This feller has more money than the national debt of Iceland.'

Now even I had heard of Hiram Firefly. He's something of a celebrity, though not in the Howard Hughes league, whose main interest in life, apart from the money he already has, is the money he is going to have. Anyway, that's the sort of stuff the gossip columns put about. I weaken shamefully.

'Oh yes. What does he want us to do?'

I can guess, but I am playing our cards carefully, mainly because we have not got many.

'He wants to meet you for a start.'

'I see.'

'Then he might employ you as stewardesses on some new

spaced-out airline of his.' I don't think 'spaced-out' is a very reassuring way to describe an airline, but I don't say anything. Firefly already owns Trans South West, an internal American airline. We used to meet their girls sometimes when we flew to the States. All white teeth and 'How are you-all doing?' Very wholesome stuff.

'Look, I don't know exactly what it's all about, but why don't you go and see him.'

'When?' I ask, a shade too fast. 'I mean we're inundated with offers at the moment.'

'I can imagine,' says Richard cruelly. He gives me the name of a smart hotel in Park Lane. 'By the way, I've sent you a cheque in the post. For fifty quid.' Our spirits lift a bit.

'Look, a friend of mine from the *Sunday X*— would like to buy your story. I've sold him your telephone number. For fifty quid. 'Bye.'

Such barefaced, shameless dishonesty and exploitation. You have to admire the wretch. And he's so good-looking with it.

Almost as I put the phone down, it starts to ring again. It's the *Sunday X*—.

'Call back in five minutes,' I say, because I want to talk to Kate. Kate hasn't got all of our conversation and she is furious. I explain what is going on.

'Anything to get away,' she says hopefully.

'What are we going to do about the *Sunday X*—'

'I don't know. They'll drag us right down the gutter.'

'Tell you what, let's sell them our story and split.'

'If we tell them what really happened, we've had it.'

The phone rings again.

'Hello, it's Jack X from the *Sunday X*—'

'Yes.'

'Richard MacGregor said you might want to talk to me.'

'We don't.'

'Well now, that's a pity, because at the moment none of my colleagues from the other crusading, deeply concerned Sundays knows your real names and telephone number – not yet they don't. Some of them are deeply worried about the scandal of air stewardesses who use their uniform for gain. A deep sense of shock is felt.'

Suddenly I have an idea.

'All right. Can we meet you this evening, at 8.0 p.m. You come here and we'll give you all the details.'

'Exclusive to us. I'll bring a photographer.'

'How much is it worth?'

'Depends. But it'll be a lot.'

'OK, see you about 8.0 p.m., here.'

'Are you nuts?' asks Kate, 'we will never be able to get another job in an airline in this country.'

'Look, darling, we won't get one now.'

'Stop saying, "Look", you sound like that bloody Richard.'

'Let's tell our problem to Mr Firefly, he'll help I am sure.

'I'm not.'

A few hours later we are sitting in Hiram Firefly's suite. Actually it's more like a re-creation of Louis XIV's court. Mr Firefly is about fifty-five, very tall, body like whipcord, thick grey hair and a slow, Western accent. He sounds like an elderly cowboy — I expect him to say, 'Heigh-ho, Silver', at any moment. Round his neck he wearing one of those boot-lace ties, fastened by what appears to be a solid gold egg.

'This here is a solid gold egg,' he says, fingering it. 'It came from the river just near the house on our ranch. It enabled my father to buy the ranch and start the Firefly Corporation.'

It is uncanny the way he reads my mind.

'There is no gold left. Just this one nugget was found. It started a gold rush in New Mexico which came to nothing. Left a lot of bitterness, but it enabled my father to buy more land very cheap. And that's why I'm a rich man today.'

He talks in a slow, drawn-out fashion, but it's absolutely hypnotic. A hugely rich man who knows it and accepts the power gratefully.

'Now you-all are probably wondering why I asked you to come here.'

Kate has practically disappeared into the embrace of a huge soft, armchair, but her head can be seen nodding vigorously. Put a bell on it, and you would have Big Ears round in a flash. Lovely girl, Kate, but she can't keep her cool in this sort of company. I sympathise. Nor can I. I'm smiling idiotically.

27

'I saw your jolly little picture story in that magazine. There was such a sense of fun about it. I liked that. I like open honest, girls. Hell, we all know what goes on in airlines I should, I own one. Well I'm looking for two English stewardesses, good-looking mind you, to work with some of my American stewardesses in a new venture. Jumbo Tours. These are going to be for the very rich only. One Jumbo Jet, with the inside completely gutted to fit individual staterooms, is being prepared now. We're gonna have an itinerary about three months – like a cruise, but this is going to be much more exotic. Stopping at three of the world's most exclusive resorts, all developed by my corporation, of course.'

Hiram Firefly goes on to explain that life for the superrich is a bit humdrum. They need new experiences, new sights and new thrills.

'Of course,' we trill knowledgeably.

His tours will supply the craving for novelty. A month in Africa, a month on a private Greek island and a month in an Alpine château, skiing. The Jet will stand by for excursions and trips. It seems to me a bit like taking a Sherman tank out into the garden to kill greenfly, but who am I to question the ways of the super-rich?

Hiram Firefly has obviously worked the whole thing out in great detail. The first tour takes off in two months' time. Over a fantastic lunch of pheasant and smoked sturgeon, he becomes quite warm.

'I like you girls. Yes. I want you to work with me. Do you agree?'

I don't bother to ask about pay or anything. We would practically pay to join, after the way he's painted it.

'We would very much like the job, wouldn't we, Kate? There just one thing you could do for us first.' I explain about the *Sunday X*—. His brow darkens. There is a low, slightly one-sided conversation with a telephone.

'One of my aides is taking care of it. Now, honey, would you like a little marron glassy?'

I'm sure I would, and I do. And a few glasses of Chablis.

'So flinty,' says Kate who's been reading, *Make yourself a cordon bleu in sixty-five parts at your newsagents now.*

I am slightly overcome by the whole situation. Out of the

window, soundlessly, the traffic roars up and down Park Lane. The park is full of flowers and leaves. One minute it's the end of the world and the next you're on the edge of a whole new one. We are to fly to Albuquerque, New Mexico, next week. We stagger into the afternoon sunshine and hail a taxi.

'Where's New Mexico?'

'Down the bottom, near Texas.'

Kate got an 'O' level for geography, so she's a great help in these matters. The climate is sunny all year round. Humidity is never high. Numerous millionaires have made their home in New Mexico owing to the excellence of the climate and the cleanness of the air. An incomparable feeling of vigour is stimulated. The guide book is issued in 1947 by the Taos Chamber of Commerce, but it is all the Fulham Library has on the subject. And after all, if there were that many millionaires in 1947, the place will be crawling with them by now. And what with all that vigour, how can a girl go wrong, as Kate so cutely puts it.

That evening the phone rings. It's Richard, yet again. Suddenly he can't keep away, it seems.

'Meet you at the Engineers. Must have a talk.'

'OK. What time?'

Kate is horrified. 'You're not, after all he's done to us.'

'I'll probably stand him up.'

'That's what is worrying me.'

'Don't be crude, Kate, after all he did make us famous.'

'Penny, I haven't dared ring my dear mother and father since yesterday because of him.' She sounds very emotional.

'Last time I saw your father, he said they hadn't heard from you for six months, so keep calm.'

'And you're going to go out with the little bugger.'

'I don't think he is.'

'You know what I mean.'

'Yes,' I say mysteriously. I suspect Kate is a bit jealous.

'At least I wasn't in the cockpit,' she says as she leaves. This is definitely a low blow, a foul, not cricket, not lacrosse, for that matter. My cheeks burn.

I find myself taking great care with my clothes and make-up. Too much, really, if you think he's only asked me for a drink round the corner. But he's got a way with him. Some people make things move, others are a very negative force. I almost feel grateful to him. Anyway, only about half a million men read that particular magazine, and they are not the sort I associate with. This turns out to be incorrect. When I get round to reading my mail it's full of letters and cards from old friends, some of them slightly funny. Most of London, and the whole of Heathrow Airport 'just happened to be looking through a magazine, when I couldn't help noticing . . . etc.'

As Errol puts it when he rings: 'I really feel I ought to see more of you, Penny.' So this is stardom. No wonder Marilyn Monroe got tired of it. So far, fortunately everyone seems to think Kate and I were just posing, which is the embarrassing thing. And I am going out with the man who conned us. I decide to teach him a sharp lesson.

But Richard disarms me by just laughing.

'Win one, lose one,' he says, as though this explains it all. 'Life is a jungle, Penny, a jungle, and I'm a winner. Anyway, I didn't come here to talk philosophy. What I want to know is, what is Hiram Firefly up to?'

'And I thought you had come to take me out.'

'That too. Now tell me what the old goat's up to.'

But I recognize a tactical advantage when I see one.

'I'll tell you over dinner. Where are you taking me?'

He takes me to a very smart restaurant in Chelsea. Everyone knows him. He kisses the waitresses. Some of the waiters look as though they would like to get in on the act too, but he just pats one of them affectionately on the shoulder and says, without malice.

'Get off, you terrible queen, you.' To my amazement this does not cause a scene. This is how the super trendies carry one. The place is full of them, the famous or semi-famous – at least they all look as though they are famous. Everyone is competing for the attention of the patron. At the prices he's charging, he should be on his knees begging their forgiveness, but he wanders around the tables, paunch creeping over the top of his velvet trousers, shaking hands and accepting compliments with a good grace. Very Latin. Pity Kate isn't here. Unordered, champagne and orange juice cocktails arrive at our table.

'That means Franco likes you,' says Richard. I've obviously gone up in Richard's estimation. There is such an air of decadence about the place. The men all rich and the women all beautiful. Certainly not a wife in sight, not with her husband, anyway. I'm glad I am wearing my near see-through silk blouse, with no bra. None of the women is wearing anything remotely conventional and they all talk loudly and say 'fuck' a lot, which surprises me at first.

The meal is delicious. I can't eat much after Hiram Firefly's lunch, but Richard falls on his as though he hasn't seen food for days.

'Been too busy to eat. Anyway, people who don't like food don't like sex,' he maintains.

Over a brandy, served I notice in a narrow, straight glass, which Richard tells me is the proper way, he pumps me about Hiram Firefly.

'Exactly who is going on these tours?'

'I don't know.'

'Look, Penny, I'll be frank with you.'

'Make a pleasant change!' I say quick as a pistol.

'Yes, yes. What I mean is, I would like to come on one of his tours. I mean if Joe Soap and his wife are going it's not much use to me but if Jackie Onassis and the Aga Khan, to name but a few, were on it, I could become as famous as Norman Parkinson. And I might be able to get a few hundred grand out of them for my movie.'

For once Richard looks a little uncertain.

'Now, now, Dickie, don't get yourself in a lather. I may be able to put in a good word for you with Hiram.'

'Don't sod about, Penny, this could be a big break for me.'

'Yes it could drag you out of the cesspit you're in.'

Richard puffs a huge cigar thoughtfully.

'Tell you what, let's go back to my place and talk about it. He gets up giving me no opportunity to refuse. Kisses all round. He signs the bill, and Franco presses a rose into my hand.

'That means he still likes you.'

'Ta.'

In Richard's gallery bedroom we sit on the bed and sip more brandy. All the lights are on dimmers, which are now very dim indeed. Elton John plays softly on the stereo. Richard is slightly preoccupied, and doesn't say much.

31

Suddenly he starts to take off his denim shirt.

'Let's get into bed, it's much snugger.'

'What can I do? He is already down to his briefs and his lean, brown body gleams in the low light. I take off my shirt and unzip my long skirt and get in beside him. For about five minutes we lie staring at the roof, while he wrestles with weighty problems, then abruptly he begins to kiss me and run his hands over my breasts. He is a man with very intense concentration; when he turns his mind to making love, he does it with the same energy as everything else. In no time at all, I am ready for him and pull him on top of me. It is brief but satisfying.

As I am thinking he is dozing off, he turns to me and begins caressing me again, this time slowly and tenderly. What a strange man he is, I think. What a lot of contrasts. I feel so tender towards him that I begin to kiss his belly, and though I very rarely do this, his prick. (What an ugly word!) He lies back and watches me, which sounds very cold and sordid, but it isn't. He is just very relaxed about this sort of thing. I often think that we make a terrible fuss about sex. Some of the things that sound quite sordid on paper are really as natural as anything when they happen. Anyway, he begins to respond in the most obvious way, and soon I am sitting astride him. The first flush of passion is over, but this is deeper and even more satisfying. He lies staring up at me almost amusedly, and begins to stroke my breasts as the pace increases. Finally, we both sink exhausted back into the bed and I sleep with my head on his shoulder.

For the first time since I came back from Australia, I feel completely at ease and with such an apparent shit as Richard. Oh well, you've got to take it as it comes (no pun intended).

CHAPTER 5

Kate and I get very excited. Over-excited really. Kate forgets to feed the parrot, which goes into a decline. But it perks up no end when a very debby girl we give it to comes to collect it. It knows a better class of person at a hundred yards. Well, the days pass in a whirl. We buy things with the remains of our fortune: I see a lot of Richard, who becomes quite affectionate in his own way. I can tell I am succeeding there, because the tight-lipped girl, his secretary, becomes more and more hostile to me every day. (Later in America, we learn the phrase 'tight-assed', which suits her perfectly.)

The big day dawns in a deep fog. This is just as well because Kate and I are beginning to have a few regrets. My regrets centre around Richard, really, but also London. You forget how lovely it can be in late summer. As Kate points out, though, there are probably more Americans in London than Albuquerque, so if you try hard you can pretend you haven't left, really, but it's not terribly convincing.

'What's the matter Penny. You're walking like a pregnant duck?' I know what she means. I can barely sit down after my last night with Richard.

'It's Richard's way of saying how much he's going to miss me.'

'I see. I see, until this evening.' Kate says unkindly.

'What about you? You've been going round town so fast the dust hasn't settled in SW7.'

This is true. Kate has been trying to see all her boyfriends in the last week. Even she is surprised at how many there are.

'Had to fit them all in, darling. So to speak. Now I need a long holiday.'

You can't take anything seriously for long with Kate, which is why we get on so well. I hate introverts. There's so much in life for the taking. Kate and I like to take it all, particularly the men.

A car picks us up at noon. The chauffeur is completely

silent. He has to sit on Kate's luggage before we can close the snaps, but eventually we get it all in the long black car.

'Good morning, my man,' says Kate jovially after about five minutes of silence.

'Good morning, miss,' he replies, poker-faced.

'Where are we going?'

'I'm not allowed to say, miss.'

We seem to be heading in a southerly direction, through Clapham and that part of London.

'Why all the secrecy?'

'Govnor's orders, miss.'

Silence.

'That is the end of another sparkling conversation, Kate.'

'I once knew a chauffeur.'

'Marvellous lovers, they say, like milkmen.'

'Fabulous. The best.'

Poker-face never even looks in the mirror, which is a pity for him, because Kate is having a lot of trouble with her new tights and is trying to take them off as we go. Although it is a big car she is making very heavy weather of it. Her skirt is practically over her head. Finally she opens a window and chucks them out, practically blinding a boy on a bicycle.

'You won't need those in Mexico.'

'New Mexico.'

'That too.'

I am feeling wistful as Peckham or somewhere slides by shrouded in fog, but soon Kate's mood infects me.

'I shouldn't think we'll need clothes at all.'

'You don't think it's a sort of flying whorehouse, do you?'

'I hope so.'

'Kate.'

'Can't be bad though, can it? Small price top pay for going to Africa and so on, with the Beautiful People.'

Kate often confuses rich with beautiful, but it's a mistake I've made myself in the dark more than once.

'Hiram says I'll be in charge of the first-class passengers.'

'You'll be lucky if you fly in the cargo hold at first, my girl. Later we might give you a stint on the vomit bags if you show promise in training.'

After about an hour's travel we turn into a gate, and then down a narrow road. The chauffeur stops the car and begins to unload our luggage. In the mist we can see absolutely nothing. I am beginning to get a bit worried, when I see striding out of the fog the most divine man. He is tall with fair, shortish hair, a light moustache and a pilot's cap. He is sporting a flying jacket with lots of zips and pockets. We stand transfixed as this vision approaches and don't even notice the wretched chauffeur as he leaves.

'Hi,' he says, 'I'm Rick Holdsworth, Mr Firefly's personal pilot.' His voice is deep and slow and easy. This lad makes Robert Redford look like the village curate.

'Hello,' we sing in unison, like a pair of over developed choir boys.

Rick takes a tiny walkie-talkie out of his pocket.

'Bring her out.'

As we watch, an airline tractor pulls a gleaming white executive jet out of the mist.

'Isn't she a beauty?'

'Oh yes,' we say.

'A Lear Jet, built to our own specification. The only one like it in the world.'

This beautiful beast is towed towards us. It looks more like a missile than a plane to me. Small, deadly and fast.

'As soon as Mr Firefly gets here, we'll be away.'

We enter the Lear Jet by a little stairway which is let down automatically. Rick shows us around. It's been done up as three rooms basically. One is a very modern study and living-room. Deep seats, all with safety-belts, a low table, a desk and a bar. One corner of this room is stacked with electronic equipment.

'This is Mr Firefly's mobile communications centre. From here he is in direct communication with all his headquarters, by telex, radio or telephone. Through here is where you girls will be able to make yourselves comfortable.'

It is the sweetest little cabin with two bunks, a tiny table and a wash-basin.

'Mr Firefly's bedroom is next door.' We are dying to have a peep, but no offer is forthcoming.

A steward comes on board and Rick and his co-pilot go into the cockpit to check the controls. The steward is an elderly coloured man who tells us he was Mr Firefly's father's servant and who now acts as butler and steward wherever Mr Firefly goes. He's no slouch at mixing a Martini, either. The gorgeous Rick is now wearing a very smart uniform and he joins us for an orange juice.

'You girls are gonna enjoy this whole darned enterprise,' says Rick in his lovely voice. It is so deep it makes the small hairs on my back tingle.

'We sure are,' says Kate, slipping into the vernacular. I know Kate and I are thinking only one thought at the moment, but Rick seems unaware of our interest.

'Yessir,' he says, 'this is gonna be one exciting time, for all of us. This is one fantastic new idea of Mr Firefly's.' His deep blue eyes stare evenly ahead, which really must be a test for any man as Kate and I are lying back in our seats with about two yards of English thigh exposed. Can he be a Mormon or a Seventh Day Witness or something like that? This great big hunk of Western apple-pie. When he goes back to the cockpit, he touches his cap and says,

'Well it sure is good to have you-all aboard.'

'I sure would like to have you-all aboard,' says Kate quietly and sincerely after he's gone, echoing, I'm afraid, my thoughts exactly.

'I bet you are really missing Richard,' says Kate, 'I can tell by that look in your eye. By your pale, sad face.'

'My darling, if you don't shut up, I'll tell Rick you're a dyke.'

'Rick, Richard, what's in a name?'

'May the best girl win, Kate.'

'Look, why don't we just split the prize?'

Before this conversation can explore the depths, which it is inevitably about to, Hiram Firefly comes aboard. An aide brings six brief-cases, one of which is chained to his wrist by a fine silver wire. They are all deposited in a safe. The cabin doors are shut, and Firefly says into the intercom,

'Take her away, Rick.'

'Yessir.'

The surge of power for such a small aircraft is fantastic. Mr Firefly smiles at us indulgently, a smile like a $100 bill folding, as it was described by William Hickey.

'Little beauty, isn't she?'

'Marvellous.'

'Yessir, this is one great little plane. But wait till you see what I've done to our special 747.'

He calls the steward on the intercom. I can't believe my ears, he's called Rastus.

'Rastus, bring us another Martini, and we'll have lunch as soon as it's ready.'

'Yessir, Mr Hiram.'

Rastus, can he really be called Rastus? Kate is trying hopelessly not to laugh. I look at Rastus with new respect. Still, he's at least seventy.

'Chicken Maryland, Mr Hiram,' he says.

'Chicken Maryland with pumpkin pie to follow, I hope?'

'Yessir, you're right as usual. Quite right.'

'That's because you always order the same menu, Rastus.'

'Well I know you get tired of this here Con-tee-nental food.'

'Doggone right I do. Too much in the way of sauces, mushrooms and cream, it's not good for a man of my age.' But he looks very well on it.

'Your father, sir, would eat nothing, not a thing but Abilene steak and grits when we was in Europe, Mr Hiram.'

'Silly old fool.'

Rastus, obviously put out by this remark, goes off and busies himself in the galley. Lunch may be what they call good ole country style food, but it's terrific. Baked clams, delicately fried chicken, creamy coleslaw and pumpkin pie or 'punkin pie' as they call it. We drink a lot of Californian wine with it, so we are glad to accept his advice to 'get some shut-eye', before we land in Philadelphia; 'like the cream cheese', Kate says helpfully as we doze off in our little bunks. Flying was never like this.

At Philadelphia, where it is now dark, we stop miles from the terminal building but immediately a tanker refuels us and we're off again into the night. No mention of customs or passports or anything vulgar like that. Mr Firefly speaks into the intercom.

'Rick, show these girls the sight from the cockpit. You go first, Penny.'

I practically break the twenty-yard dash record. Captain Rick motions his co-pilot out of his seat and I sink in beside him. His strong hands hold the joy-stick lightly.

'Flies itself, really. Those are the Alleghenies below, and

37

there's Scranton, Pennsylvania.' He leans across me and it's all I can do to stop myself giving him a big hug and kiss. It's marvellous, just the two of us in the cockpit with the night all around; the sky is lit with stars the way it is so very rarely at home. Rick explains the controls and the special equipment they have on board. It's enough to boggle the mind completely. Fortunately, I'm not really listening to the words, just the sound of his deep, quiet voice. I try not to think of the last time I was in the cockpit of a plane. I cross my legs firmly.

We fly on ever further west. America is so vast. By now you would have flown over three European countries and we still haven't even got to the Mississippi, so Rick explains. He obviously loves the wide open spaces. Europe, he says, is too cramped for him, and Mr Firefly feels the same, though he likes it. But they are both men who feel most at ease when they can't see another building. The first settlers used to travel until they could no longer see the smoke of their neighbour's chimney, which on the plains is a long, long way. And that's how he feels. I am used to thinking privacy is your own room, on alternate nights if you are lucky, but I understand what he means.

'Kate coming up,' says the intercom, breaking the spell of the prairies as Rick describes them to me.

As Kate comes in, I stand up and kiss Rick lightly on the cheek and say in my sexiest voice.

'Thanks, Rick, that was marvellous. A truly wonderful experience.'

Both Rick and Kate look a little startled. Mr Firefly gives me a drink and tells me more about his new venture and what we will be required to do. It's miraculous. We only fly about three times a month, and for the rest of the time we act as sort of hostesses and advisers.

'Camp counsellors,' Mr Firefly calls us. I'm not complaining. He is a remarkable man, I think as we talk. So sure of himself, so relaxed, and yet full of ambition and energy. It shines out of him like a naked light. I wonder if he fancies Kate or me. We would be in a difficult position if he did, enjoyable possibly in the short term but not really much use in the long term. He strikes me as the sort of man who has as much use for sentimentality as Genghis Khan. Once we were no more use to him, that would be that, I am sure. Pity really, because he's extremely attractive in an older sort of way, but best to keep away from it, if possible. I can't help speculating, however.

Dinner is served as we cross the Mississippi. Rick joins us.

'Who's minding the shop?' I ask.

'Hell, this thing flies itself. You just point her for home and fold your arms. Pete can handle her anyway. He should be able to, he flew two hundred bombing missions in Vietnam.

'Now I feel I'm coming home,' says Hiram, 'this is where the great wagon trains set off to explore the West, my grandfather amongst them.'

We can't see a thing below, but his enthusiasm and warmth are infectious. Perhaps it is enthusiasm that enables the successful to influence other people, and to become successful. That and money, of course.

'Just think. It took my Grandfather five months to reach Albuquerque. And it will take us just five hours. That's science for you – that's aviation. But it's not enough. Nossir. Science gives you help, but it doesn't give you answers.' His eyes are burning bright, almost fanatical. Kate seems mesmerized. At least if Kate stops eating for ten seconds, it comes to much the same thing. And old Rastus is a dab hand in the galley.

Rick and Mr Firefly seem to have a father and son relationship; even though Rick treats him with great respect. It is obvious that they have a deep, mutual regard. Mr Firefly, it turns out, sponsored Rick through college and into the Air Force after his parents died. His parents worked for Mr Firefly as chauffeur and cook. That's something which is so American, and we learn later, much more Western that Eastern. Class differences don't seem to exist, though there is great respect for wealth and achievement.

'Well, I had better get back to the controls, we'll be landing soon. Thank you for dinner, sir, see you in the morning, girls.'

'He never leaves the plane until it is safely in the hangar. He loves this plane. But he's too modest. He was decorated for bravery five times in Vietnam, even though he hated those goddam bombing missions.'

We land at an airfield on the Firefly Ranch, near Albu-

39

querque. 'Near' is a relative term, I explain to Kate, because it's actually seventy-five miles away.

A line of huge black cars is waiting on the tarmac. It looks a bit like a funeral cortège. Each one is as big as a hearse in England.

'You and Penny go in that one, the Lincoln, to the guest house, and we'll do the invitations in the morning. You must be fair tuckered out.'

Rick waves from the cabin door. 'Take it easy,' he shouts,

'Or anyway you can get it,' says Kate gratuitously.

The huge car whisks us off into the night. We've been doing a lot of whisking lately.

CHAPTER 6

We awake to glorious sunshine pouring into our room. This guesthouse is really a separate cottage built in the Mexican adobe manner, about a quarter of a mile from the main complex of the Ranch. On one side we look over a little whitewashed courtyard with a table and chairs under an old tree. It is paved with what looks like pink granite. On the other side is a huge swimming pool, about the size of Datchet Reservoir, as Kate says. And the back of the cottage looks out over miles of empty scrub with a low range of purple mountains far in the distance. The buildings of the ranch itself are low and Mexican-looking too, built round a vast square which is planted with trees and cactus.

As we are dressing (jeans, we decide, are appropriate) and I'm struggling a little to do up the top of my Lothars, a horse pokes its head in the window. I get the fright of my life. It's a very fierce looking brute. I peep nervously out – sitting on top of it is Rick. He looks even better in chaps and a stetson than in flying gear, if that is possible to imagine.

'Hija, girls, sleep well?'

'Yes thank you. Take that nasty thing out of our bedroom.'

The horse is giving the curtains a little chew to see if he likes them. He does.

'Just been taking the old horse out for a canter. He sure has missed me, got as fat as a hog.'

I love horses, though in fact the closest I've come to them is giving sugar to police horses. This one is an altogether different proposition. It spits out the curtain. Fussy about his food, too.

'What's his name, Rick?'

'Morning Star – he's the finest stallion in the South West. A cutting horse.'

'Is he a communist?' asks Kate.

'We don't hold much with Reds in this part of the world. Breakfast is served in the chuck house, other side of the pool. All the folks are dying to meet you, so hurry now.'

With this he canters off. It's so Hollywood, I almost expect him to turn in the saddle and wave before he disappears into the middle distance.

All the folks turn out to be Hiram's family, his quite good-looking nineteen-year-old son, Brad, his wife Laura, Hiram's dishy assistant Jim and various other friends and members of the staff. They all seem to be one big happy family, though I dare say there are things going on that the eye doesn't see. Thank heavens.

Breakfast is a feast. Brunch, they call it. Rastus, now back in his element, is supervising the grilling of huge steaks over a charcoal fire. Hiram Firefly, dressed in immaculate Western gear, is very concerned that just the right amount of barbecue sauce should be applied to each steak, steaks that might have been cut off the inner thigh of an elephant. Plates of blueberry pancakes with maple syrup keep appearing from nowhere.

After lots of 'Pleased to meet you, ma'ams', and 'How are you-all doings', we make a start on the breakfast. The whole scene is too much to take in. Everything is on such a big scale. The ranch alone is the size of Buckinghamshire and Northampton together half a day's drive across. And all the people are so warm and friendly to us, so interested in us, and so keen that we should like New Mexico. We do, already.

'Work starts next Monday, girls, so enjoy yourselves while you can,' says Hiram. 'We're having a real Western barbecue tonight, some of the folks from these parts are coming over. Maybe Brad will show you the flying museum or perhaps Rick will take you for a ride. Apart from myself, he's the best horseman on the ranch.'

They laugh at this last remark, but I notice nobody is disputing it.

'I would love to get on a horse,' I say as quickly as is decent.

Jim and Brad take Kate off to see the flying museum. Hiram has collected planes, can you believe, for years. In a huge hangar, Rick tells me, are fifteen vintage planes, all of them serviceable, and most of them in use in the ranch.

'I'll take you up for a flight one day, but let's get out in the desert now.'

Rick chooses a huge horse for me from the stable.

'She may be big, but she's old, wise and as comfortable as an old armchair, and just as safe.'

He helps me strap on some chaps over my jeans, fits me up with a Western hat and heaves me into the saddle.

'That's it. Just you hold on to that big knob there and you'll be OK.'

For a moment I think he may be making a joke, but his blue eyes are already scanning the horizon eagerly, perhaps looking for Indian smoke signals, who knows? His stallion is cantering about, prancing and snorting, but I am reassured to see that my animal takes not a blind bit of notice. She's as steady as a rock and sitting in the big Western saddle I don't feel frightened at all.

'Come on, Doris,' I say.

'She's called Blaze.'

'For me she's a Doris. Good girl. Steady now.'

As we wander pleasantly along what seems to be a dried-up river bed, Rick gradually gives me a few tips, like how to stop and turn, which I imagine could be handy at times.

'Neck rein pressure is what these horses respond to, because when you are roping you gotta keep your right hand free for the rope.'

I don't see me and Doris doing a lot of roping in the near future, but Rick has such an encouraging way with him that I begin to feel quite confident.

'Do you want to try a little canter?'

'OK, but what do I do?'

'Just hang on and leave the horse, she'll follow me.'

When Doris is going up, I am going down and it feels as though I'm landing on a pile of rocks. I can only take a few minutes of this torture.

After Richard, I almost say, I am used to it. Richard. He seems a whole world away and yet it was only yesterday, or perhaps the day before, that I saw him last. I feel a little guilty because he hasn't crossed my mind once since we got aboard the plane.

We leave the river bed and head towards a low group of hills.

'We'll dismount there, have some coffee and stretch our legs.' This is welcome, because I am feeling very weak after all the unaccustomed exercise. When we get to the hills, Rick tethers the horses, and carries the saddles over his arm to the crest of some boulders, piled up like giant potatoes. We go through an arch in the rocks and I see the most beautiful, clear pool. The water is ice cold. Round it are a few small trees, lots of ferns, and soft green grass, like a lawn.

'Rick, why didn't you tell me? What a lovely place.'

'It's my little secret. The water comes out of the ground up there and disappears just there. As clear as you could wish.'

'It's fantastic. Do you come here a lot?'

'Only with people I think will appreciate it.'

I most definitely take this as a compliment. Rick has a little fire blazing merrily with a canteen of coffee on it, and we stretch out with our heads on the saddles, just like in the movies.

'Mr Firefly knows about this place, but he's left it as it is. It's a sacred place for the Indians and a watering-hole for the desert animals. One day I'm gonna have a little cabin in these hills, and that will be the last the world ever sees of Rick Holdsworth.'

'It sounds a marvellous idea to me. Can I come and visit the hermit occasionally?'

'It's very hot lying in the sun.'

'Can I have a swim, Rick?'

'Sure, but be careful, the water's ice-cold.'

'You won't look, will you?'

'I will.'

'Well it's not that I am shy, it's just that I'm so pale.'

I go behind a rock and slip off my jeans and shirt. Shall I go in in my bra and pants? They will dry quickly in this sun. I decide to compromise and keep just my panties on. They are not the biggest panties in the world, but the water is crystal clear and as I hardly know the man, it seems prudent. The water is so cold it takes my breath away. My nipples ache for a moment or two until I get used to it. Rick seems to be taking very little interest, so I swim around quite boldly. He is lying on the grass by the side of the pool wearing just his jeans and boots. His bare chest is lightly covered with fair hairs. Can he be asleep? I swim up to him and grab one of his feet. He dives into the pool, boots and all, and ducks me.

'That will learn you.'

'Oh Rick, help, I'm drowning.'

He puts his arms around me, my breasts squeeze against his bare chest and he kisses me as we go under. We splash about like kids for a while and then get out on to the grass. Rick kisses my wet mouth once more and rubs my breasts dry with his checked shirt.

'I hear you have a bird in England called the bluetit?'

'Yes.'

'Well I have never seen two such fine specimens.'

In the short while I have known Rick, this is the first time I have ever heard him be even faintly rude, and it's a great load off my mind. My nipples are a bit blue, but with Rick's attention and the cold water, they are standing up very firm and erect.

He kisses me deeply and my tongue slips into his mouth. I lift my hips almost involuntarily as he pulls down my panties. He drapes them on a bush. We have a slight problem getting his wet jeans and boots off, but overcome it, and I feel him firm and large, with my fingers. He caresses me skilfully to readiness and eases himself on top of me. I draw him into me with a deep sigh. It all feels so good, the sunshine, the swimming and now this beautiful, beautiful man. By the time he's finished, I am sobbing with happiness.

'Are you all right, honey?' he asks tenderly.

'I always cry when I'm happy.'

'My God you are beautiful,' he says. I am lying on my back totally content, my legs apart and the sun caressing every inch of my body. No wonder people who live in sunny countries are so randy. I mean it's so much easier to make love in the middle of the desert than on a 19 Bus, though I tried that once as a schoolgirl and the spotty lad and I ended up in the bus sheds in New Cross. But I digress.

Rick has the sun haloing behind his hair, and is looking at me as though he means it. After a while we have another swim this time totally nude. Our clothes are drying a bit by now, and we set off to the Ranch. Rick has water squelching in his boots as he does some rather fancy galloping, stopping and turning. He explains that quarter horses have to be kept in constant training. He has been known to ride in rodeos, as well as all his other accomplishments. I just clop along with a rather silly smile on my face, I am afraid, thinking of one of his more private talents. If he could bottle it and sell it, this boy would make a million.

Still, millions seem to be taken for granted around here. Round the pool we have a bite with Laura, and lots of highballs, as they call a cocktail. Kate tells me she has been up in a bi-plane with Brad, who, it seems, is a rather lecherous youth.

'How was your morning?' she asks.

'Quite good fun.'

'And Rick?'

'He's smashing. A marvellous rider.'

'I'll bet,' she says, implying so much. I don't try to deny it.

'Jim looks nice?'

'He's great, but unfortunately Brad was playing the boss's son a bit heavily. I wouldn't have minded having Jim tie my seatbelt for me, but young Brad there is like a bloody octopus.' Young Brad is staring at Kate from the other end of the table rather intently.

'Still, he'll be OK when he grows up. It's just that I've got past the adolescent bit.'

'Yes, when you were about twelve.'

'Now, now, Penny, you weren't such a slow starter yourself. But he could be a problem. When I was changing for a swim, he was peeking through the window, I am sure.'

'What did you do.'

'I just carried on. I thought maybe he could get it off his chest.'

'I think it's your chest he's interested in.'

'Did you have a good morning?' asks Mr Firefly.

'Wonderful, thank you, I just can't believe how lovely it is here.' This pleases him, but it is also true.

'Well, you girls spend the afternoon by the pool if you like, resting up, because we're having one big party this evening. And your time-scale will be all screwed up by the flight over. You better believe me, now.'

Rick has to go and work on the planes, so Kate and I get into our bikinis and lie by the pool, long drinks close to hand. Mrs Firefly never swims, she says, because her complexion cannot abide the sun. Mine can. It's lapping it up. Kate and I doze comfortably in deck chairs with umbrellas attached. Kate loosens her bikini top to get an overall tan, and I notice Brad peering at her from the chuck house. He catches my glance and disappears.

Still, who can blame him? Kate's bikini is tiny and despite

46

her large front, the rest of her is very slim and lithe. The poor boy probably has never seen anything like it. Thinking about crystal clear water and the adorable Rick, I float off into a deep untroubled sleep.

Late in the day we consult Rick about what we should wear to the barbecue. He says we should look English, everyone will love us, which sounds promising. Outside, near the chuck house, an ox has been roasting for two or three hours. The sun is going down in a blaze of colour, and I realize those sunsets you see at the movies are for real – vivid yellows, reds and pinks. Kate wears a pair of satin trousers and a small halter top, and I wear a short, simple white dress, without a bra.

Compared to the other guests, who are piling out of the biggest, longest, fattest and most ornate cars you have ever seen, we feel like orphans at a Buckingham Palace garden party. Jewels sparkle, the men wear white tuxedos, the women long dresses, and they all carry around half the output of De Beers as though it were Biba plastic beads.

'At least we'll stand out.' Kate is already doing that, though she's getting a lot of competition. Plunging necklines, with huge rocks nestling at the top of the cleavage, seem to be the order of the day. But everyone is so friendly – even the women, which is a new experience for us. They think our accents are 'just cute', and they think that Hiram's taste is 'as good as ever', and that our 'Carnaby Street dresses are just darling'. In short we soon feel quite at home. It's a question of enthusiasm – everyone is doing something, everyone is excited about something – so different, I think, from poor old England, where one day we will probably just go to sleep for ever.

As the highballs begin to flow, so conversation gets louder and the laughter more raucous. Delicious smells are coming from the ox-roast where the inimitable Rastus is doing his stuff; floodlights under the pool are turned on as the sun finally disappears. Rick arrives, in a beautiful white linen suit, without a tie, which makes him look like something of a hippie in this company. Jim follows shortly and the two of them lead us off to have some supper. We sit at little tables dotted around the swimming pool. Rick produces a bottle of best vintage champagne which we polish off in a trice.

'Penny!' says our Kate.

'Yes, darling.'

'I don't want to embarrass you.'

'No.'

'But you really shouldn't wear black panties with that dress.'

'Is it that obvious?'

'Yes, dear. Particularly with this light.'

This makes me feel a bit uncomfortable, to say the least. I thought I was getting some funny looks. Anyway, I excuse myself and go over to the guest house to change my knicks. As I'm stepping out of them, someone grabs me from behind, squeezing my breasts and pushing his hips into me. I think it's Rick and try to turn round, laughing. But the figure holds me very firmly in his hands kneading me through my thin dress.

It's Brad, the boy octopus, and he's terribly drunk. He probably thinks I won't tell on the boss's son. What do I do? I am half undressed and it's no good shouting for help.

'Now, Brad, there's a good boy. Just relax.' He's grinding away with his hips like a randy woodpecker. I decide to try and fool him. He turns me round and seizes me in an almost desperate embrace. One hand is up my skirt, the other round my back.

'Come on, honey, let's get on the bed. You European girls know all about it. I saw you looking at me by the swimming pool.'

I feel a bit sorry for him, even in the midst of my predicament. He's been drinking enough to kill a horse by the smell of him.

'Come on, honey, give me a kiss.'

His flushed adolescent face is thrust against mine. I kiss quickly and start to undo his trousers.

'Come on then, big boy, show us what you've got.' He hastens to help me and as his trousers are round his ankles, I push him on to the bed and make a run for it knickerless. I would find the whole thing funny, but for the fact that he is the boss's son.

'What took you so long,' says Rick.

'I had a little bother with Brad.'

'What sort of bother?'

I explain, but don't make it sound too awful.

'Jesus, I'll beat that kid's head in.'

48

'No you don't,' says Jim.

I laugh it off, but Rick is none too pleased. I wish I had not said anything now. At this moment the wretched Brad comes staggering by, his trousers restored. He looks a bit sheepish, if you can imagine a very drunk merino. Rick sticks out a leg and gives him a nudge. It is so fast that he's walking one moment and in the pool the next. My only worry is that he'll drown. The guests think the whole thing is hilarious and soon people are being thrown in wholesale. Women in diamonds and long dresses, men in tuxedos. It's a riot. I go in, followed by Kate. When I come out, I am virtually naked, but by now the whole party has degenerated to such a degree that nobody cares. Jim steps into the water to rescue Kate who is being torpedoed by an elderly gentleman with a rose in his teeth. Soon Kate and Jim are kissing, Jim in immaculate tuxedo, his bow-tie still firmly in place, and water nearly up to his armpits. We hand them a bottle of champagne.

They really enjoy a party in this part of the world. Someone brings out a shotgun and shoots a rubber swan to smithereens. Hiram presides over the proceedings amiably. I notice nobody has pushed him in.

'Having a good time, honey?' he asks. 'I said it would be one hell of a party.'

Two men wearing only pants and bow-ties are shooting at bottles with huge pistols. They don't seem to hit them too often.

'You kill more than five of my cattle out there and you ain't gonna be invited again, my friends,' says Hiram, but he is quite unconcerned. They blaze away into the night.

The band strikes up. Soul music. It's an incredible sight to see some of the richest people in the world bopping away like kids, most of them wet and one girl actually topless, her small breasts bobbing like corks on the wave. Champagne is literally flowing, as one faction takes on the other with bottles of Veuve Clicquot.

I dance with Rick, who is clearly much admired by the ladies in this neck of the woods, but he had eyes only for me this evening and I feel very happy about it. My dress is clinging like a second skin and I have nothing underneath it, but I don't care – it is that sort of night. Rick is wearing his dripping suit with great style, his fair hair plastered about his head, a cigar in his mouth. We dance like dervishes for about an hour before he leads me away to the guest-house.

All the action and, in a funny way, my encounter with Brad, have made me feel very excited. As Rick unzips my dress, I fall on the bed and pull him on top of me.

'Do it to me, Rick. Now. Come on, come on.' His broad lean shoulders loom above me.

He's also excited, and in no time we're lying exhausted in each other's arms, only separating to sip champagne. We are still like this as the sun begins to rise over the sage. Rick slips away, and I fall into a deep, deep sleep.

Dare I say, a perfect day?

CHAPTER 7

The rest of the week passes in a flash. Or even faster. Kate and Jim are having a very meaningful relationship, she tells me.

'Meaning what?'

'Meaning that he's a terrific lover, and a lovely bloke.'

We compare notes in girlish fashion. Jim and Rick are both pretty busy during the day, but we get taken all over the ranch by Hiram and his family. 'Ranch' really doesn't do justice to it. It is the big country itself, with three other ranch-houses on it, two airstrips and two thousand miles of road, or track. So far no oil has been found, but there are prospecting teams turning up all sorts of other minerals. One day Hiram takes us into Albuquerque to see the sights, which include the Firefly Health Resort, Forest Ridge, which Hiram explains is the most expensive fat farm in the whole world. It is all built around an indoor swimming pool which a Roman emperor would envy, under a giant glass dome. Every guest has an individual set of rooms, each one furnished differently and there are six staff to each guest.

The fat, the rich and the old come to stay and leave, still fat and old, but not quite so rich because it costs one thousand five hundred dollars a week, but for that you eat your grapefruit each day off, a 'customized set of Limoges china', explains Barbra-Ann, the lady in charge. She is in her late thirties and so energetically healthy in her emerald green leotard and I begin to feel as though my life of decadence must be slung like a neon sign above my head. She surveys me with professional interest.

'You're in pretty good shape, but then you're young. When you get to twenty-six or so, you'll have to start working on it.' She makes it sound like a religious duty.

Hiram tells us he is going to send any stewardesses who get overweight here for two vigorous weeks. I wonder if it is a warning, but he says no, just wanted us to have a little old look about. Kate understands it quicker than I do.

'That lady is his mistress,' she says of Barbra-Ann.

'How do you know?' But I realize she's right. Hiram tells us he set her up in business some years ago. One of her masseuses is coming on the flight. There will also be gambling, with roulette and craps. I have no idea what craps may be, but don't think I had better ask as we are just about to tuck into a jumbo plate of jumbo prawns in the country club. Shrimps, the man calls them, but each one looks like a slightly stunted lobster to me. If I go on like this I am going to be the first candidate for the fat farm.

'Now you girls are gonna be senior stewardesses, as you've had international experience. You'll be in charge of the other girls and report directly to my director of passenger services, Mr Dobermann. Feel free to make suggestions. The first flights will just be shakedowns with reporters and travel writers from all over the world. So when anything goes wrong, you analyse the problems and let us know.'

Our pay, he tells us, will be $450 a week, which will be pocket money as we will be living at the Ranch when we are not on duty. Riches, wealth.

'Anyway, work starts Monday, so you haven't much time left for enjoying yourselves.'

We put our backs into enjoying ourselves, though I must say with those two bronzed cowboys, Rick and Jim, our backs spend a lot of time horizontal. Kate even begins to hint that Jim may be a bit over-sexed. Kate Goodbody may have met her match. Can this really be true?

'I've never known anything like it. He's at it day and night. Underneath my tan, I'm a pale, tottering wreck.'

For a pale wreck, she's looking pretty good, in fact I would say she's thriving on it. It's a funny thing about sex, for a girl anyway, the more you have the more your appetite seems to increase. At least that's my experience. I am not looking forward at all to going away from Rick next week as he'll be back on normal duties. Kate and I have lots to do in the training programme, and we will be at the Firefly headquarters at the main airport.

'Oh, Rick,' I say to him that evening, as we sit on his bed, 'I'm going to miss you.'

'Well it will only be for a few days at a time, honey. I'll drop by the airport whenever I get a chance. I'm often down to the headquarters of Firefly Aviation.'

I stop him talking about the job, his only weakness, with a

well-earned kiss. Rick has one like, which in the beginning I am a little doubtful about. That is what they call a 'blow-job' in America. Now in England it's not unheard of, but here is seems to be an obsession with the men. Rick lowers me on to the floor and I take him into my mouth. He loves this, and I begin to find that what gives him pleasure turns me on too. Perhaps that's love. Still, I do prefer the face to face missionary approach generally. After a while he lies back and I get on top of him. The motion gets fast and faster and I begin to cry out wildly. The approach of our separation affects both of us and we make love almost savagely as if to remember something especially important and exciting.

Monday, the first day of what Hiram calls 'familiar-ization', and Rick flies us the hundred odd miles to the head-quarters of Firefly Aviation. It's a gleaming building set beside the main airport terminal, but it has its own terminal and its own hangars. We are introduced to Peter Dober-mann. Later we hear he's called Dobermann Pincher, amongst his colleagues and for reasons which soon become obvious. He is kindness and courtesy itself, however.

'Well, girls, I am the head of the passenger facilities div-ision, and to be honest with you from the start, I'm gonna need a lot of help from you. A whole lot of help. I know all about international flying but our girls here have only flown internally within the States. So I'm gonna be relying heavily on you to help them and to train them.'

He shows us all round the building and then takes us over to a 747 hangar. One particular jumbo is painted a shocking pink with FIREFLY SPECIAL stencilled boldly all over it, with the Firefly emblem, an eagle in flight, in the tail-plane.

'Come aboard.'

As we climb the steps he asks, 'What do you think?'

'It certainly is different!'

'Wait until you see the inside. It's been designed by David Zarachsy. This will blow your mind.'

Indeed it does. The inside of the plane has been com-pletely gutted. It is more like a suite of rooms in a luxury hotel. Not a solitary seat of the normal sort, but three huge reception rooms, a dining-room and a cocktail bar above, up the spiral staircase.

Dobermann takes us down a wide corridor.

'Every passenger will have his own stateroom and all the girls will have a cabin, two to a cabin. There's yours.'

He shows us a darling little room, which, we are chuffed to see, has 'Senior Stewardesses' and our names stencilled on the door. Our cabin is quite small but it has a wide bunk each and lots of hanging space, which is one of the things that really bugs me about normal aircraft. You are expected to look cool and fresh, but your uniforms are always stuffed into a tiny cupboard.

'Of course you won't get a lot of chance to use those in flights,' says Dobermann, giving Kate's behind a friendly tweak as she reaches up to look at the top bunk. Still, he's an amiable sort of fellow, though he seems quite worried about the first flight. I must say, it seems like a job that can only give him headaches. Stewardesses are not the easiest people to look after – flying rotas, passenger complaints, often quite unjustified, not to mention female illnesses, boy-friend troubles, menus, catering, terminal facilities – all this is his responsibility and now this new venture on top. He is going to come on the first trip with us. When you think about it, perhaps pinching is like a nervous tic for him. I don't get away without a few nips myself before the end of the tour of the plane.

The plane is so imaginatively done up, with every conceivable luxury, that only now does the nature of our job really hit us. We had thought, I suppose, that it was really just a rather posh airline, everyone travelling first class. But this is another league altogether.

'Well my department are used to dealing with the public who use our airline. We try to keep them happy and fed and comfortable. But of course we've never had contact with them for three months before. I am now a cruise director as well. Anyway, we seem to be managing well.' He goes on to explain that this is really money invested in the future, in the Firefly resorts, in new forms of transport, in the belief that we have only just started on the age of travel. I find it all very fascinating.

Back in his office, he shows us the uniforms. Even more than the plane, they are a joy. Just the sort of thing most stewardesses would opt for if anyone ever consulted them. Kate and I have special uniforms in line with our responsibility, for formal wear. These consist of a soft, cloche

54

type of hat with a simple but very elegant suit and underneath a silk, V-necked blouse. The whole effect is very sexy thirties. The skirts are either midi, with boots, or rather short, with flat shoes. Very practical, and very lovely. And there are cheesecloth smocks, very sexy for in-flight, worn with very snug trousers. So snug that Kate can't get hers on. They look as though they've been fired at her like a plastic shrink wrapping. And as for the cheesecloth top, it's jutting out like a shelf. Mr Dobermann seems delighted with the results, though he realizes the fit could be a little improved.

'Mr Firefly said you were healthy looking girls. Try these on now.' 'These' are alternative wear for hot climates, simple long shifts, with rucked necks!

'We had them all designed in Paris. Real clothes with a slightly uniform look, that's all. Do you like them?'

'I think they are wonderful.'

'Of course, you won't be able to wear that black bra with these shifts.'

'No, I can see that.'

'Now to in-flight arrangements. We have a French chef with four assistants, and he will be preparing individual meals to requirements. You girls will not do any waiting yourselves, but will take orders and make sure that all the other girls get the message.' He shows us some sample menus, with Kosher, vegetarian and dietary variations.

The next day we meet the other girls. And I must say all are very pretty, young and eager to please. One is particularly pretty, called Bridget, and of course Kate and I treat her a bit more frostily than the others. But they are so keen to learn from us and so pleased to be complimented that we almost stop worrying about possible competition. Actually, just one night away from Rick and I'm not as philosophical about parting as I should be. With these chicks around, we're going to have a struggle on our hands to get at the available men, so Kate and I decide. They are the pick of the stewardesses from Firefly's airline, and although none of them has flown internationally, they are quick to learn. They want to know, most of all, what the men are like in Europe and Africa. I've never been to Africa, but Kate flew London-Nairobi for a while, so she's soon telling them all about white hunters and their weapons. She lays it on a bit thick, I think.

'Kate, what garbage that was about safaris and lions.'

'I know. All I ever did was shack up with a tea-planter in the New Stanley Hotel. Still, you soon pick up all the bush craft you need in the bar.'

'Well you shouldn't go on like that.'

'Penny, if we are going to get these girls' respect, we will have to lead from the front.'

'Yes, but they will think international flying is all parties and men the way you go on.'

Kate's expression speaks louder than words. She looks at me in pained amazement. That's obviously exactly her definition of international amazement. Trouble is she knows, and I know she knows, that it is my definition too. In fact we took up flying for one very good reason – men. But I feel we should behave in a slightly more dignified manner in our new role, and I say so.

'The young gentlemen tell me you screw in a terribly dignified manner, Miss Sutton,' says Kate smoothly. The idea is ridiculous, and of course I realize that it is hopeless trying to be serious with Kate around. Thank goodness. For one or two moments I was letting my position go to my head. So we talk about customs regulations, health certificates, climate, hand out leaflets and grooming and beauty aids, prepared by Barbra-Ann. Not that any of these girls need help, but we are trying to create our own, glossy, international look, with imported make-up and the newest hair styles, free and natural instead of piled up on the head like a little cowpat, as recommended by all the best airlines.

Beauty classes are being conducted at Forest Ridge by Barbra-Ann with the help of a Swedish beautician. Later that day we all troop off to the sauna and have half an hour, followed by an exhilarating massage. The sight of ten of us naked in the sauna would drive most men out of their minds, I imagine, but we get that jolly hockey sticks feeling and it turns into quite a romp with poor Bridget going head first into the cold plunge. Bosoms bounce, the fur flies and we begin to feel like a team. My skin is so clean after the sauna and the facial that I hardly want to put any make-up on at all. I feel so beautiful and so healthy, I just wish I had someone to put it to use on.

As if by magic, Jim and Rick appear in the cooling room at Forest Ridge. My heart leaps.

'Right you are, girls, let's go.' Kate and I bid the others goodbye and the boys lead us out conspiratorially.

'Have a good time you-all.'

'Don't be late in the morning, teacher,' says Bridget pointedly

'It's like the bloody fifth form,' says Kate, but she's laughing all the same.

'You're looking terrific,' says Jim.

'Where are you taking us?'

They won't tell, but we pile into a beach buggy loaded with good things and we head out into the desert. The sun is setting in that fantastic fashion, almost vulgar, it has out here.

'We are going to do some desert trailing, kid,' says Rick happily. How he loves the open air. When he's flying he is calm and relaxed, but serious. Out here he's like a child. He yells and shrieks as we tear down narrow rutted tracks, deeper and deeper into the desert.

'We were fantastically lucky to get down here with Mr Firefly, who has some business with Forest Ridge this evening, so you little Limeys are also in luck. In fact I'd say we are all some of the luckiest people in these parts.'

The word 'parts' checks Kate for a moment. She looks up hopefully. Actually she and Jim are like a pair of vacuum cleaners locked in mortal combat, but from what I can see she is holding her own, or his, perhaps.

Jim is singing like a banshee and I give him a big kiss, which practically amputates his ear, we are bouncing so much. He turns to me and seizes me in a wild embrace. The beach buggy roars on down the trail, masterless for a moment. We hit a rock which hurls Jim and Kate into the back of the beach buggy, but they are not hurt. We all think this is hilarious, and Jim produces a bottle of Tequila, and a lemon.

'Take a suck of the lemon and a big swig of this,' is his excellent advice, 'and you will feel like Pancho Villas's aunt.' I don't know a lot about Pancho Villa or his aunt, but if she felt as sexy as I do after a few gulps, then she was a very lucky old teapot.

We stop near a pile of boulders, the sort of thing Indians use as cover in movies, and by the time night falls, Jim and Rick have a fire going, some coffee in a canteen and some steaks sizzling satisfactorily. Nobody is paying much attention to the steaks. Only three feet from Rick and me, Kate and Jim are going on a voyage of discovery all over each other. I catch a glimpse of one of Kate's magnificent boobs in the firelight (she was always something of a girl guide), a small portion of it about to disappear into Jim's mouth, which makes me titter, if you'll pardon the pun.

Meanwhile, alert readers will have guessed that Rick's strong fingers have not been idle. I rather like this sort of fumble and grope – it makes me feel like a thirteen-year-old again.

'Now, now boy scouts, you've let the coffee boil over,' I say. We all break off, rather like the interval in a wrestling match, and eat a delicious meal. Char-boiled steaks are something Americans rave about, and I can see why. There is no comparison with restaurant steaks – still, perhaps the Tequila helps. The sophisticated way to drink it is with salt and lemon, but by the time I have had about four of them I could drink the stuff with chicken manure and it would make no difference. Rick gets his guitar out of the buggy and we sit around the fire singing songs like *The Old Grey Mare* and knocking back the Tequila.

'Wonderful stuff, Tequila,' says Jim. 'In the morning you don't have a hangover at all.'

'That's because you're dead long before daylight.'

'Over the border down there, in Old Mexico, men go blind from drinking this stuff.'

Rick decides to express himself musically with a rendition of *Down Mexico Way* and we all join in enthusiastically if rather untunefully. It is so peaceful out here in the open, miles of nothing around us.

'Can you imagine doing this on Wimbledon Common?' asks Kate.

'If the police didn't nick you for vagrancy, the rain would get you.'

'Great town, London,' says Jim incoherently. 'Great li'l ole town.'

But London could be a million miles away. I can't even conjure up a picture of black taxis and red buses. Nor of Richard.

'Sssh!' says Rick, 'there's a coyote.' We listen intently, and I feel a shiver all over me as we hear a distant howl.

58

'That means the moon will be out soon.'

Almost as he says it, a slice of brilliant moon appears above the horizon. The coyote howls as though he is in pain.

'The Indians say that the coyote carries the souls of their dead ancestors in him. He is talking to them ... What we would call a medium, really.'

Rick is such a mine of information. It is still warm, but we huddle closer to the fire and Jim puts on another log. I feel an almost unbearable affection for Rick. His dream of a little house out in the hills and a quiet life making cornbread and feeding chickens appeals to me so much at this moment that I am tempted to propose to him. But he's strumming and singing quietly to himself, and I don't suppose he would accept me anyway. He is really the sort for some platinum blonde cowgirl, with lots of money and a pink Cadillac.

Still the thought troubles me as we drive back to town through the empty, moonlit sage brush.

CHAPTER 8

'You've got that stupid smile again,' says our Kate as we make our way to the stewardess training in the morning.

'What stupid smile?'

'That sort of imbecile look of satisfaction.'

'Thanks a lot. Or thanks a bundle, as they say around here.'

'That's OK. I know you were thinking of England when you acquired it. You're a sort of raving ambassador. In fact I am thinking of putting you in for a Duke of Edinburgh's award for exports.'

Kate has this really irritating habit of making jokes in the morning. It's true I'm feeling a little stunned this morning, but then Rick told me he has to go off to Europe for a few weeks with The Boss. All very unexpected.

The week passes very fully. We seem to be welding the girls into a wonderful team. The following Monday we are to have a press flight, which will be what Pincher calls a shakedown. Old Pincher is winding himself up into a state of frenetic activity. He becomes almost frantic as he explains to us the details of the flight schedule. Twenty-five of the world's top travel and feature writers. Take-off from Albuquerque 11.0 a.m. Fly to San Francisco, 4.30 p.m. Refuel, take-off for New York City, cabaret and dinner, followed by touch-down at JFK at 11.0 a.m. Twenty-four hours of hell.

'Mr Firefly himself has chosen this as a testing first flight. These people are going to be tired and irritable and you're going to have to keep them happy. They are some of the world's greatest gourmets and bon viveurs (he makes it sound like a perversion) and you've got to satisfy them; they have travelled in everything from a mule cart to the Queen Elizabeth, and you've got to make them think this is a new, fresh experience; they must all go home and write about it. Girls, there is a grave responsibility upon you. I want every one of these men and women to go home full of enthusiasm for our new venture.'

We are practically in tears. Chins and bosoms stuck proudly out, these girls will die for their country.

The journalists duly arrive, and a motley band they are too. A marvellously attractive, middle thirties gentleman in an elegant safari suit catches my eye.

'Good morning, sir, this stewardess will show you to your stateroom and welcome aboard.' Bridget waits to show him to his room. 'Cocktails will be served in the forward lounge after take-off.'

'Thank you very much, mademoiselle. You are charming, most charming. In France we call it le sex appeal. That is droll, non?'

He follows Bridget, his eyes fixed to her trim little hips as she leads him off. An enormously fat English travel and food writer appears; I know his face from television, and he is immediately happier when I tell him. At the other door, Kate is greeting passengers and sending them on their way with great verve. I begin to feel quite relaxed.

When they are all installed in their cabins, the girls do a quick change into smocks and sit down for take-off. We will be leaving in twenty seconds, says Pincher over the PA system. Unfortunately nothing happens. A technical fault. One hour's delay.

'For Chrissake get the booze out,' says Pincher, his cool destroyed. All the girls look at Kate and me, sick with apprehension. What a terrible start!

'Now girls,' I say, 'get in there and get them smashed. And get those silver dishes of caviar out right away.' They scurry off in all directions.

'You have the best speaking voice,' says Pincher, 'so make the announcement.'

'Ladies and gentlemen, owing to heavy traffic over the Rockies we shall be serving drinks now and delaying our departure by one hour. Anything you may desire will be provided by the staff. Please come into the forward cabin if you wish.'

I try to keep the quaver out of my voice. In fact there is no need to worry. Travel writers are cynics of the worst sort, but they like a drink and they like a pretty girl, so we muddle through quite well. The Frenchman has Bridget by the arm and is whispering in her ear. I just catch him saying, 'I am a very frank man. That is my habitude. But it is your decision entirely.'

All the journalists seem to know each other, and the champagne and caviar vanish at an alarming rate. One young man, from the *New York Examiner*, is already tucked up in bed as I pop my head in to see if he needs anything.

'No I had too much last night. Well, OK, see if you can fix me a bullshot. And wake me when, and if we take-off.'

Fortunately the bar knows what a bullshot is. It's cold consomme and vodka. Very nourishing. With little problems like this solved we begin to calm down and take in our guests. The girls are responding to the crisis magnificently, and although this lot are very demanding, we hardly have to refuse a request. Kate is rallying the troops in the forward lounge, and I am looking after the back.

'Those smocks are very sexy,' says the fat Englishman, who must think I am a fan. 'Are they very comfortable?'

'Very comfortable. You can't imagine how easy they are to work in.'

'Haven't I seen you before somewhere? You and the other girl over there, the English one?' He is looking intently at my breasts as though seeking a clue – they are pushing out the smock rather cheekily.

'I don't think so.'

'Well, get me some more Beluga Caviar while I think where it was.'

By the time take-off is possible, we seem to have won most of them over. Jean-Paul Belmondo is monopolizing Bridget a bit, but I don't say anything as yet. He seems to be very persuasive, with those expensive, crinkly eyes. The poor girl has obviously never met a French Romeo at full throttle in Albuquerque. I must warn her nicely. 'Above all, remember that these are people, your friends – not passengers who are going to get off at the next stop,' Hiram warned us when he met the whole crew last week. I can see the pitfalls ahead.

Even these blasé travellers are impressed by the aircraft. Each girl takes one or two around and shows them all the special features. The thing that intrigues them most is the idea of a personal stateroom. Perhaps some of the possibilities they see for them are not strictly above board, but then I must say Kate and I have already had the same thought.

Kate and I meet briefly.

'How's it going?' I ask.

'Christ, one of my lot is a German flasher. He's already trapped poor Lindy in his cabin and exposed himself.'

'What did she do?'

'Well, she said trying to look in his eyes, "the chief stewardess will be round in a moment to see you," and fled.'

'Good girl, is she all right?'

'Oh fine, all she said was that German sausage seems to be bigger than hot dogs. What do you think that means?'

'I've no idea at all. What cabin is he in, maybe I can find out?'

'Tssk, tssk.'

We pass around the lunch menus, movies are played on colour monitors, backgammon boards and card tables are produced a bridge four gets going for enormously high stakes, and we serve coffee and cognac to some Swiss gentlemen, who are beginning to loosen up a bit.

For the ladies, one of Barbra-Ann's staff is on duty for facials and hairdos, and for the men another for massages. Almost nobody looks out of the windows and nobody at all goes to see the controls of the plane. They have all done it all before, more than once. Jean-Paul has disappeared to his cabin and there is no sign of Bridget. She hasn't fallen so soon, I hope. I make a discreet knock and he calls me in. She is not there, I am pleased to see. He is wearing a white flannel dressing-gown, negligently exposing a lean, brown thigh and reading *Paris-Match*.

'You are very kind to call upon me. At ze moment I 'ave everything that I could desire except for a pretty girl like yourself. Oh yes, you are thinking, 'ow direct is 'e, non, but I am very frank. When I admire a girl, I do not 'esitate to put my feelings to 'er.'

Hello, I've heard this before somewhere, but he is terribly attractive.

'If there is anything you want, sir, in almost any other line, you have only to say the word.' He kisses my hand and gives it a little squeeze.

''Ow charming you are. We shall see. Goodbye.' No wonder poor Bridget is looking a little confused. Those hazel eyes are magnetic. Probably got a fat wife and three kids back in Paris, but this isn't Paris. I find Bridget and say as pleasantly as possible, 'No favouring special passengers, now, even though he is smashing.'

She just laughs and moves off, little hips grinding rhythmically to serve a guest She really is far too sexy for her own good, I tell Kate, who says:

'Yes, just like you.' I take this as a compliment at first but then I begin to wonder.

The serving of lunch goes almost without a hitch. The passengers can either eat four to a table in the restaurant or in their cabins. Most prefer to eat together. Fresh Maine lobster and Texas T-bone steaks are the most popular choice but some go for the sea-food pastry cases and pressed duck. Liqueurs flow in a tide. The German flasher stays in his cabin and exposes himself to two more girls. We all want to have a look, but by the time I get there he's fully dressed and stays that way. Perhaps he's had enough. By the girls' account, he can't afford too much of that business without running a grave risk of loss of blood in the rest of the body. He is stoking himself up with rosti, a kind of finely chopped Swiss potato. Maybe when I come back the boiler will be burning again.

'Ja, one more bottle of Niersteiner, then some more Sacher Cake, yes?'

'Yessir, make yourself comfortable. I'll be back to see you in a moment.' Perhaps a flasher likes to shock and we've taken the fun out of it for him because when I come back he still has nothing to display. Oh well! Of course I don't let on and Kate is determined to have a look, particularly after my lurid description of this phantom Teutonic member. She comes back with an even more exaggerated report than mine.

After lunch the masseuse does very good business. She is a very pretty little Chinese girl, who wears white shorts and a T-shirt – she smiles constantly in a rather demented fashion. I must say, I could not face a life-time of running my hands over wobbly flesh, but she seems to like it and the men certainly like her.

One shift of girls goes off for a 'freshen up' as we call it, which involves a break for half an hour and a change into afternoon and evening uniform; it's then that I notice that Bridget is not in her cabin. Now only Pincher, Kate and I know that all the cabins are monitored into Pincher's room,

64

because he wanted to be sure that we could check on all these sort of problems early in the game. I select a switch and on a small screen see the whole of Jean-Paul's cabin. Bridget, wearing only her pants, is between Jean-Paul's legs. Mercifully her blonde, bobbing head is obscuring most of the action, but he sits in his chair, eyes closed, for all the world as though he were having a manicure. I am in something of a dilemma, because as senior stewardess I have clearly found one of my staff in dereliction of duty, but as Penny Sutton I am dying to see what happens next. What happens next is that Pincher comes in and closes the door quietly. We watch the whole thing unfold. Bridget is obviously anxious about time passing, because very soon she is on the bed and putting her neat little bottom to energetic use, and then almost as fast, she is dressing. Jean-Paul seems to be asleep.

'I think we have seen enough, don't you?' asks Pincher as she goes out of the door.

I am afraid there is a catch in my voice as I say, 'Yes, more than enough.'

'We'll have to fire her. There are going to be enough temptations in three months without falling for them all at once.'

'I suppose you want me to do it, on account of I have such a nice speaking voice?'

'No, honey, that's my job.' He seems to be looking forward to it. The atmosphere in the room is somewhat close and steamy, one way and another. I leave, and on the way to my room see poor Bridget.

'Hiya,' she says with a white, white smile.

I can't help wishing it had been me, but as Pincher says, we can't have everybody hopping into the sack with one another at the slightest excuse. I go to our cabin to change and tell Kate to get back on duty. I really need a cold shower, but there is not time. Kate is dying to hear all the gory details, but I remind her that she has a whole section to look after.

'Like a lance-corporal in the WRAC,' she says.

'More like a madame in a brothel, with this lot.'

After San Francisco I begin to get a bit worried. We've let the greyhounds out of the traps a bit early, what with all the champagne before take-off, and they're getting dangerously close to the hare. One woman writer has to be helped to bed by two of her male colleagues, and although she's not going to win any beauty contests, the two men do not emerge from her cabin. And we haven't even served dinner yet. Pincher reads my mind.

'What they do in there is their own business. We certainly will not use our TV monitor!' Alas!

'Quite right, Mr Dobermann,' I say, as though the thought had never, could never, enter my head. 'For staff matters only.'

'That's the idea, Penny.'

He looks very smug about it.

'We have on board enough booze to keep the whole of the goddam Red Army stewed for a year,' says Pincher, 'and the barmen tell me that they have nearly finished the lot. I'll have to get the captain to radio Chicago for some more. Jesus, you would think these guys had never seen a drink before. In fact they are the world champion spongers, goddam freeloaders every one of them. Look at the bastards.'

It is getting rowdy. I have to release one of my girls from the grips of the Swiss, who have become positively extroverts.

'Give me a kiss, liebchen,' says the fatter one. I get away, but practically leave my bra behind in his stubby fingers.

'Mr Dobermann, let's give them dinner early; that way at least they will be stationary for a while.'

He agrees and we begin to circulate the menus.

'Bags I go to the lady journalist's cabin,' says Kate.

'OK, but I want a full report.'

When I get to the fat Englishman, the TV personality, he says,

'I remember. Now that you've changed into that blue number, I remember.'

'I am afraid I don't know what you are talking about.'

'I remember. Yes indeed I do.'

'What would you like for dinner, sir?'

'How about the chicken surprise,' he says, running his hand right up my thigh. Only the thought of his influence on public opinion restrains me from bashing him on his reddish nose.

'I'm afraid that is not on the menu either, sir.'

'Yes, yes, you and your friend. The one with, how shall I say, the larger apparatus.'

'I'll come back for your order sir, if I may.'

'Yes do. Perhaps I will have a pair of plump little partridges, who knows?'

Jean-Paul is now sitting playing backgammon with an American journalist. By the look of things the American is being fleeced. But he doesn't seem to mind. As I lean forward to take his order, Jean-Paul says, quite loudly:

'After Chicago, in my cabin, OK?' and turns to his companion, 'Two dollars a point, OK, ça va?'

The funny thing is, if I had not seen him in action once already today, I would have been tempted. He is so self-assured and continental. I am afraid the sort of person who has only to lift a finger and waiters come at a canter, appeals to me.

'Something to build up your strength, sir,' I ask innocently. 'It's been a hard day. Can I recommend the steak tartare?' He gives me a funny look, which I attribute to his having misunderstood my remark.

The rest of the flight is a shambles, but most enjoyable. One of the Swiss throws a plate of rosti all over the other, and all hell breaks loose. Food begins to fly, the German flasher does a streak the length of the plane, warmly applauded. By the time the lights go down for the cabaret, all the girls are in mortal peril. I stop bothering about casual gropes, and save my energy for the attempted gang-bangs and rapes, which are frequent. Heaven help you if you wander down the corridor towards the cabins. The front lounge becomes the discotheque, and we dance away like crazy. The service becomes self-service, but as Pincher says,

'They sure are enjoying themselves.'

Bridget is nowhere to be seen, but then she is technically off duty until 5.0 a.m. The fat Englishman has me in a very firm embrace as we dance, obviously fascinated to learn more about our little photographic venture. I deny all knowledge of it, but that does not stop him. He is practically swallowing me by the time a faster record comes on. I give him the slip and try to clear up some of the mess. It's quite hopeless. Pincher retires to bed, saying,

'They sure are enjoying themselves, aren't they? I am sure Mr Firefly will understand. I sure hope so.'

So do I.

Kate tells me that the lady journalist has completely passed out.

'Before she went, she kept calling me Alfredo!'

'She must be really pissed.'

'And the two blokes have gone. There they are.' My God, they are going into their cabin with Bridget. That girl must have the stamina of a horse.'

'Oh well, she's for the chop anyway, so she might as well go out with a bang.'

'Or two.'

The Frenchman comes up and slides an arm around us both.

'In France we are more, 'ow shall I say, frank than your poor Englishmen. I would like to be ze meat in your sandwich. Come with me.' Despite his clear, Charles Boyer voice, he is completely, leglessly, drunk. He is still inviting us to dinner at the Tour D'Argent, with a little, 'ow shall I say it afterwards, when he begins to crease up. We help him to his cabin, loosen his shirt, hang up his jacket and trousers on a hanger and put him to bed. Kate is all for undressing him completely, but I am sure Pincher will be watching. I blow the concealed TV camera a kiss, and we leave.

I am too tired to resist when the young man from the *New York Examiner* leads me on to the dance floor. Anyway he's quite attractive, so I rest my head gratefully on his shoulder and we dance dreamily for ten minutes or so. He begins to press himself to me, not the least shy about what's obviously going on in his trousers. I feel a stir in my thighs and rub gently against him.

'Come to my cabin,' he says, urgently.

'I would love to,' I say, 'but really I can't.'

'Why not?'

'Well, it's against the rules. You're a most attractive man, but I would be fired immediately if I did.'

He is quite attractive, but even without the possibility of old Pincher looking in, I don't think I would consider it. Perhaps it's Rick's influence over me. We continue to dance very close for a while. I am beginning to get a bit stirred up so I excuse myself before I get into mischief.

Very few people are still up. One of the Swiss is lying on the floor, but none of the girls has volunteered to help him because he has already ripped Jeannie's dress off when she

tried. I clear up as much as I can with the two girls still on
duty and then go off to our cabin. Kate is sleeping the sleep
of the dead, and I set our little clock for 7.0 a.m. which is
only three hours away.

When we touch down in New York at eleven, there are
some pretty ashen faces. Not Jean-Paul of course. He looks
as though he has been at a rest camp for a week and is
drinking champagne cocktails. Not Bridget either. She looks
so young and fresh in the morning light, that you might
think she was hoping to do her 'O' levels soon.

We bid them all farewell, and they all thank us, kiss us and
press addresses on us like old friends.

The Englishman says,

'I liked the one on the cockpit best. Goodbye, dear.'

CHAPTER 9

Well, we stumble on with the training programme. I must not exaggerate — it goes quite well really, except that one thing puzzles me. Bridget is still with us. Pincher never refers to the incident again, so I say nothing. After all human weakness has always been one of my favourite pastimes, and I am beginning to like Bridget. She is a genuinely sweet girl engaged to be married to a football star at the local college. No self-respecting American town is without its college, and no self-respecting college is without its football team. One day we watch the mastodons playing. Quite amazing. There is a mighty eruption for five seconds, after which everyone is flat on their backsides,then they all line up to do it again.

'Quite a lot like sex,' says Kate unnecessarily.

Bridget is beside herself with excitement.

'Look, there's Chuck. Attaboy Chuck. Go baby. Kill him. Way to go baby.'

All the players look alike to me, but I must admit it has a sort of primitive power about it. Kate asks what's supposed to be happening.

'We're gonna make a touchdown. Go Chuck, go baby.'

Huge thighs churn. Heads crack together, and suddenly the whole stadium goes berserk, with cheers, chants, and trumpets.

'Just like a party in Earl's Court when the beer runs out.'

So Bridget is still with our particular team. Her golden hair frames a cute smiling face, and her devotion to big Chuck, who is about six feet five, is truly touching. I can hardly believe it is the same girl, particularly when she and Chuck talk about all the children they are going to have over a cosy hamburger and Seven-up. Chuck doesn't drink, of course, because he's in strict training. Fortunately one or two other members of the team are less dedicated, and they take us off to a restaurant and bar, where we all get happily plastered. These brutes are very keen to get us back to their fraternity house (sounds like the Mafia), but we make our excuses and go back to our apartment without them.

Because next day we are to welcome passengers and set off for our first stop and our first trip. Otherwise, as Kate says, it might have been fun to see what they have under their padding. We wake up bright and early, not a little nervous and get ready to meet the first passengers on the maiden voyage of the Firefly Special. We will be in Nairobi the next morning and then out to a private game reserve, owned by the company, of course, for three weeks. Meanwhile the plane will fly occasional excursions to other parts of Africa for those who are interested in other parts.

At the Firefly Corporation Headquarters, all is feverish excitement. A special departure lounge has been decorated for the launch, the Press, Radio, and TV are there, and Mr Hiram Firefly is going to wish us godspeed and say a few well chosen words at the same time. Kate and I are interviewed by WBF, the local TV station. Actually Kate is interviewed, while I try to get in the occasional word. She bags most of the interview, and most of the screen too, but the latter is an accident of nature and I do not hold it against her. I have not talked to Mr Firefly for days as he has been in Europe but he finds time to squeeze my hand and say,

'Rick will be back soon. We'll be joining you out in Africa in a week. Now you pitch right in there, honey. This whole thing is gonna be fantastic.'

He has a way of making the heart beat quicker with devotion to duty.

'Thank you, Mr Firefly. Thank you, Hiram.' I say stupidly.

Rolls-Royces, Lincolns, Cadillacs begin to arrive with the first guests. Some arrive in private planes. Many are locals, Texans and South Westerners, but others are from New York and the Coast and others from as far as Europe. One couple come up to me with the unmistakable accents of Lancashire.

'Hello dear. We're Mr and Mrs Birtwhistle from Blackburn. I'm glad to see the old country represented 'ere. Come along lass, let's get on plane.'

It immediately falls into place. These are the winners of the English newspaper competition for a Jumbo Jet Tour. Mr and Mrs Birtwhistle of Blackburn, of course. I warm to him in his Gannymac and sandals, worn like the true purist

71

with grey socks. She has an Instamatic, which, in this company, is like entering the Monaco Grand Prix in a Hillman Imp. Kate shows them to their cabin and comes back nearly hysterical.

'He's stripped to his string vest, and she's got her feet in the bidet already, with baths salts. Lindy is trying to find him a Newcastle Brown. She thinks it is some sort of coloured gentleman he's after.'

'Well, it was well advertised as the trip of a lifetime. See the world's most expensive resorts. And all as the guest of the *Evening Echo*. All you have to do is name the greyhound and fill in a suitable caption for what the hare is saying.'

'Probably saying, bah gum, I'll be buggered if they catch me.'

A porter comes bearing a mountain of luggage, followed by a beautiful lady who looks as if she's held together by fine wires.

'Hi,' she says, 'I'm Amanda Greer, and this is my luggage.'

'Welcome aboard, Miss Greer. This young lady will show you to your stateroom.'

'Amanda Greer, patron saint of the plastic surgeon,' explains Pincher. 'There is not a thing on her body that isn't phoney. Some say the dimple on her chin used to be her navel.'

There are only twenty-five passengers, or guests as we are supposed to call them, but the rich don't travel light and it takes us a while to get them stowed, show them around and then meet Mr Firefly.

He is so masterful and assured with them it takes the breath away.

'Hiya, folks. Many of you know me. I hope you will all know me as friends at the end of this exciting experience in leisure. I have put together this enterprise to provide something totally new and totally stimulating for people like you – people like me. We are the advance guard of the future. Our staff have been chosen from the finest in my airline and from even further afield. Our aim is to give you the experience of a lifetime.

'Mr Dobermann here is in charge of the cruise, and this Jet is your second home for nearly three months. I hope to see you all in Africa shortly. Now have a good time, won't you. Goodbye and Godspeed.'

We take off as though He were on our side, exactly on cue. One very well-known German-American actor, Jens Brandenberg, is sitting in one of the alcoves with two girls. He is fifty-five at least, wearing a flowered Indian shirt with his silvery hair tucked back over his ears. We begin to serve drinks and snacks, and these two girls who look about seventeen, but a very corrupt seventeen, select a programme of cartoons on a monitor and settle down happily drinking Cokes. Jens watches them indulgently, as though he is very glad he doesn't have to help them with their homework today. He's very proud of them obviously. I introduce myself to him and he in turn introduces me to the girls, Helga and Chantal. Actresses, who are going to star in a film financed by him after the trip; this way they will know each other so much better at the end of three months. Sounds reasonable to me. The girls sit close together, one skinny arm entwined with another, so they already know each other quite well. Helga has long, absolutely straight, black hair and Chantal has fair, straight hair, though much shorter. Jens has a very relaxed way with him, possibly the result of having made $20 million, so Kate suggests. As far as Kate is concerned, money is the greatest relaxer in the world. I must say, I am inclined to agree. I mean if you prefer the 34 bus to a chauffer-driven Rolls, you must like to suffer. And would Jens, if he weren't rich and therefore powerful, have two beautiful teenaged girls with him at his age? And they clearly make him happy.

Pincher in a rare moment of poetry, describes them as fallen angels. Most apt.

We gradually get to know the other passengers. They are mostly middle-aged, but there is a rather strange young man, rumoured to be the manager of famous pop-groups, who doesn't say a word. He just sits and stares at a TV screen from behind dark glasses. With his Afro hair, only about two inches of his face are left exposed, and that little looks fascinating.

I offer him a drink, and he gives a short, high giggle.

'Look, I'm not into stimulants lady. Bring me a carrot juice – I'm the macrobiotic freak on your list.'

His voice is slow and resonant, but that is all he says for

the next few hours. Lindy has obviously heard of him and she is always just around the corner. He never moves, never goes near his cabin, never utters a word. He just stares at that screen; even when the same movie starts again, he doesn't select another channel.

The knowledge that we are all going to be together for a few months makes the atmosphere quite different from any other flight I have ever been on. You actually feel like getting to know all the passengers, not just the ones who may be stopping off in the same hotels as you on arrival.

'To be honest with you, dear, I've never been outside England before,' says Mrs Birtwhistle. 'Now my daughter Janice, she's a proper little traveller. She has been to Majorca twice and Ayebizzer twice. She likes Majorca better than Ayebizzer. Better night life. Gracie Fields lives in Capri, you know, which is thereabouts. Gracie were born in the 'ouse next door to our brother Tom's first wife, you know.'

I fill up Norman Birtwhistle's glass for the second time. He is not the least overawed by the company, though Madge is doubtful.

'Come on, lass, have a glass of mother's ruin.'

'But it's three-thirty in afternoon, Norman, pubs are closed even.'

'Not this one, Madge, not this one,' he says sloshing back his champagne. 'Champagners, champagners, champion stuff, champagners is champion stuff,' he sings in a good imitation of George Formby.

Later he brings out his ukelele and sings away like a man possessed. Madge is persuaded into doing the Hokey Cokey, her dress held high above her knees, which are themselves held in support stockings. They break the ice so effectively that before dinner everyone is chatting away like old friends. Old Norman is the star turn, and so simple and unaffected in the company of the rich that you would imagine he did it every day. Madge is quite overcome by drinking Martinis all afternoon and retires to bed. But not Norman. He has appointed himself social secretary by the time he's had six more glasses of champagne and is trying to organize a raffle on the result of the 2.35 at Doncaster, which he assumes everyone is as committed to as he is. Mrs Perlmutter and husband have sixty-two horses in training in England and some hundreds in America and France, so Norm gets on famously with them, co-followers of the Turf. Two bob doubles, he tells them, are his speciality, and they listen incredulously.

Meanwhile, Jens and his two fillies emerge from his stateroom looking in dire need of a refreshing drink. Kate is dying to find out what is going on there, but our TV monitor has been taken out now that training is over. So she can only speculate.

'He must have an awful lot of stamina,' she says.

'Perhaps he just likes young girls around.'

'Perhaps, but I think there is more to it than that.'

'And from your tone of voice you are going to try and find out.'

'Well he is very good-looking isn't he?'

'Yes, he looks just like Anthony Eden.'

'If you can imagine a hip, German version of him.'

Jens is playing backgammon with the two girls, sitting between them. They loll affectionately over him, as he tries to explain the game to them. So slim and young and yet they eat like piranha fish. Their little mouths are both painted purple now, and their finger-nails too. They chatter away in German or French with equal ease.

Norman and the Perlmutters have now opened a book on all major race courses the world over, after some discussion about the relative merits of Chepstow and Saratoga Springs. Chepstow wins. We have to get the captain to radio for the results every day, or put them on our telex. Norman is quite unconcerned that the minimum bet seems to be about a hundred dollars. After all, as he points out, a poor bookmaker is as common as a Mohammedan Pope. Mrs Perlmutter is trying to learn the Hokey Cokey, while Mr Perlmutter tells him about his entry for the Kentucky Derby.

'Jesus,' says Pincher, 'if it goes on like this, we'll all be croaked in a week.'

Later that night, Pincher's little secret emerges. I am doing my last rounds: only Rip, the pop group manager is still up, staring at the screen, when I see little Bridget creep into Pincher's cabin. She sees me and shrugs. Now I begin to understand why she is still with us. Naughty old Pincher. But she may well kill him, that child. I sit down next to Rip.

'Do you want anything, Mr Mathews?'

He does not reply. He is staring at the screen, which is playing Last Picture Show for at least the fourth time to my knowledge. He just sits cross-legged on a sofa as if he is doing yoga.

'I'm doing yoga, lady.'

'Oh, I'm sorry. I'll leave.' Yoga has always struck me as being a bit religious, and you don't chatter to people while they are praying, do you?

'Don't go.' Suddenly he begins to talk.

'I'm a junkie,' he says. 'At least I was. After they dried me out they decided I should go on a trip to get away from all my friends and all the possible sources of dope. That's what I'm into right now, so bear with me, can you?'

He tells me in his strange, monotonous voice how it all happened. He was involved with music from early days at High School but never made it as a performing musician and so he became a manager and song writer. One of his early groups and early songs made him a millionaire and ever since he's made more and more money.

'But, like, after you've cracked that, man, it's a drag. All I ever wanted to be was Mick Jagger. And now look at me. Eight million in the bank and a junkie.'

'The eight million sounds OK to me, and you're not a junkie any more.'

'You are a good kid. But listen baby, this dope is finish. I'm gonna die soon, maybe tomorrow, maybe in two years and what's eight million to me?'

He seems so lonely, so isolated that I feel I must help him. But what can I do?

'Listen, if there's anything I can do to help, you've only got to ask.'

'Well ever since I got back from the funny farm, I've been having these terrible nightmares, that's why I don't go to my stateroom. If you would come and sit with me until I go to sleep, maybe I would be OK.'

I go with him to his cabin. He lies on the bed, staring totally absorbed at the ceiling.

'Come on, Rip, get into bed.' Like a man in a dream, he obeys. And then he begins to cry like a baby, this beautiful, successful man – a musician and an artist and a businessman reduced to this. I try to comfort him, lift his head and put it in my lap. He clings to me, absolutely distraught. I have never seen anything so frightening, so deeply disturbing.

Strange as it may seem, I slip off my uniform and get into bed with him, wearing only my bra and pants. He's pitifully thin, and when he buries his face in my chest, I take off my bra and clutch him to me as a mother might a baby. His tears pour all over my breasts as he sobs. After about half an hour he seems to be asleep, and I leave as quietly as I can. Just as I am shutting the door, he says.

'You are a good kid, may your karma be good. For ever.'

When I explain to Kate what happened, she is a little cynical.

'I see, then you thought you just had to comfort him anyway you knew how.'

'Yes.'

'And then you got undressed.'

'Yes.'

'And then deep concern turned into raging passion.'

'No, no.'

'Penny, you're slipping.'

CHAPTER 10

As I help the passengers off at Nairobi, I reflect on how right
Hiram has been about this sort of venture. These rich, blasé
people (Norman and Madge excepted) are like a school
outing now. We are to fly in two zebra-striped Lear Jets to
Mula Mula Game Reserve, the world's most exclusive private game reserve, and they leave the Jumbo sadly as though
they had lived there all their lives. Most people leave a plane
with nothing but pleasure.

'Perhaps it's because they are pissed,' says Kate un-
charitably.

'Well, they're not all pissed. I mean there are a few who
are sober, I am sure.'

'Jumbo Dypso Tours, these should be called.'

Kate and I have to help Rip off ourselves. He's shaking
like a leaf, but says he really doesn't need a doctor, just a
little cold turkey.

Already the ground staff are loading luggage and equipment into a Firefly cargo plane, which is going separately to
Mula Mula. The sun is very hot, but Kate tells us that it is
never too humid in the Highlands. I'm glad of my new
cotton shift, anyway. Local reporters gather to take pictures
of us all, and an official from the Department of Tourism
makes a very flowery speech, which no one understands,
least of all the man who is translating.

Rip pats him on the back.

'You're a great cat, Sambo.'

The official asks for Rip's autograph for his children.
Sweat pours off his forehead as he tries to write his name. He
gives the official a copy of a new album he's produced and
written, not yet released in the States. The man is over-
joyed.

I find my first glimpse of Africa very exciting. It's so
primitive, so wild and so beautiful, not least of all the people
who are tall and thin, with skins like polished oak.

The local Firefly man upstages Pincher completely, but
it's not surprising as he's wearing shorts, a safari shirt and a

hat trimmed with leopard skin. Pincher, by contrast is looking a little blotchy and unwell after his labours, where this
man is brown and handsome. Ted is his name.

'I would like to welcome you all to Kenya. And more
especially to Mula Mula. This is the world's most exclusive
game reserve and we believe it is an experience you will
never forget. You can lounge by the pool, go game-spotting
in our open jeeps, watch lions feeding every night from our
tree house, or for the more adventurous go for walks with our
fully qualified white hunters. Not all of our white hunters
are white!' he says with a smile, 'but they are all very experienced. Our flight to Mula Mula will take only forty minutes
in these Firefly Mark 2 Lear Jets. Jambo.'

And off we go. I just gaze out of the window in awe. We
circle Mount Kilimanjaro, still capped with snow, and head
north. Pincher is being excessively friendly to me for some
reason, not unconnected with Bridget, I imagine and he
keeps touching me on the thigh as he points out the sights.
Still, he is a wonderful organiser. All this has been his work,
and so far it has gone like clockwork.

'Penny, listen honey, there is one thing I want you to do.'

'I know,' I say, 'fire Bridget. Because of my nice voice.'

'No, no, it's not that, but you're right it is about Bridget. I
want you to talk to her and find out if she's on the Pill.
And if not, order her to get on it.'

'The way she carries on, she would be the mother of trip-
lets if she weren't.'

'Penny, we're gonna be on this thing for months, honey,
and I don't want that kid getting pregnant.'

'He's a very big boy, that Chuck, Mr Dobermann, he
could make a terrible mess of you.'

'Now, Penny, don't get sassy. She told me that she's a
Catholic and the Church does not allow her to use birth
control.'

'OK, Mr Dobermann, I'll try and help you. On one con-
dition.'

'What's that?'

'That Kate and I get our own bungalow at Mula Mula.'

'That's not on the schedule, but I do happen to have one
that's not taken. As senior stewardesses, I think you're en-
titled to a little privacy. I certainly do. Good, that's settled.'
He gives my thigh a final stroke.

Mula Mula is a dream. We come in over the mimosa trees and land rather bumpily on a sliver of tarmac in this wilderness of green. For a moment, I think we are being attacked. Trucks, landrovers and jeeps rush at us from every side. A tribe of warriors in lion skins beat their shields and dance, chanting fiercely.

'Just a little welcome we lay on,' says Pincher. My goodness, those brown bodies. They leap and prance and shout.

'No wonder they do so well at the Olympics,' says Kate. The dance comes to an end and they hurl their spears into the nether distance.

'That was the Masai dance of welcome,' says Ted, 'not to be confused with the war dance.'

The ferocity of our welcome has sobered up one or two of the guests sharply. Each party is assigned a beautiful, thatched bungalow covered with bougainvillea. The little village is situated overlooking a river called in Masai, the Crocodile. There don't appear to be any fences, I notice, except around the trees and shrubs.

'Keep the hippos off,' says Ted casually.

I am beginning to warm to him. He and Pincher run through our duties here, which are almost nil. We just have to do the rounds every morning and make sure that everyone is happy, bright eyed and bushy-tailed. We also book any excursions to other parts of Africa, and register any special requests. In the evening we make sure that dances and gambling go off as planned. We knew all this in advance, of course, but the place itself is so breathtakingly beautiful and the idea of being in the middle of nowhere is so exciting, that Kate and I can't absorb it all at once.

Ted shows us round, more 'familiarization', a favourite word with the Firefly Corporation and he introduces us to the five White Hunters. Two of them are Kikuyu, but they are all members of the White Hunters' Association, and all of them no longer shoot, not officially anyway. Our little bungalow, or 'rondavel' as they call it, is deceptively simple from outside. It's thatched in the African manner with reeds from the river and has a huge bedroom a verandah or 'stoep' overlooking the river, and a bathroom and a breakfast room. It is air-conditioned and there is fresh fruit, iced water and a fridge full of drinks just waiting. The other girls all live in one long low building, rather like a dormitory.

Lunch is served in the open air in a 'boma' which is a round fence of reeds, something like a mat on end. We all sit around in a circle.

'In the evening we have a huge fire here,' says Ted, 'and the Hunters boast about their experiences. The biggest bloody liars in Africa, but it goes down well with the Yanks.'

Ted gets up to speak,

'Ladies and gentlemen, now that you are here I hope you will love it as much as we do. Most days we get up very early and do our game-spotting by jeep. Or if there is anything special you want to see, you may go by light aircraft. One hunter is assigned to each five of you. After lunch you may do as you please, swim or go for a walk with a guide or just sleep, then in the late afternoon we go to our unique tree house to watch the lions feeding. We come back here for dinner in the boma, and then there is gambling and dancing. Although it is quite safe, we do ask you to stay in the camp at all times unless accompanied and we also ask you not to leave the lighted paths at night. Our special interest here is conservation, and we have re-introduced many rare species to this area. Now enjoy yourselves – Mula Mula and its staff are at your service.'

Norman has already wandered off. He doesn't believe there are crocodiles in the river, but soon changes his mind.

'Christ, I saw one, big as a bloody ironing board floating down. Them things could take yer head off at one snap. Perhaps we should organize crocodile races, Ernie,' he says to Mr Perlmutter, who laughs mightily. He thinks Norman is the greatest thing since sliced bread. They order a jeep and a hunter and head off down a track, with a shaker of Martini between them and Madge and Mrs Perlmutter enveloped in a cloud of insect repellent, behind.

Kate and I decide to go for a swim. In fact all the girls do, and I seize my opportunity to talk to Bridget. She is wearing the tiniest blue bikini over her brown, slim body; though her breasts are quite large, she looks about fifteen.

'What is it, Penny?'

'I need to have a word with you.'

'Have I done anything wrong?' she gazes at me, blue eyes so anxious.

'No, love, you have been terrific. It's just that I have to ask all the girls about certain aspects of their private lives which concern the company.'

'Do you mean me and Mr Dobermann?'

'Yes, well not directly. All the girls have to be on this trip for a few months, and we don't want any pregnancies or abortions which would upset the folks back home, do we?'

'Oh no. Abortion is completely wrong. It's against God's law.'

'That's right, Bridget, so I want you to tell me straight if you are taking any birth control measures.'

'Oh no. That's also one hundred per cent wrong.'

'Look, darling, Mr Firefly has personally asked me to see that all the girls on this trip have the Pill, and he's a Jesuit.'

Two lies: how did I get myself into this?

'So you see me before dinner and I'll give you some to be going on with until you can see the doctor and get a pre-scription, OK?'

'Well, if Mr Firefly said so.'

'He did.'

'Well then it must be OK. Thank you, Penny.'

Can this girl be putting me on? I mean she makes Kate and me seem like vestal virgins, and yet she's not on the Pill. Somebody must be on her side.

'That Ted is pretty terrific,' says Kate. All the girls seem to fancy him.

'Well, he's like the head boy, isn't he?'

'Or a football star,' says Kate unkindly. But it's all water off a duck's back as far as Bridget is concerned. She is lying on her back in the sun, her arms and legs spread out as though she were expecting big Chuck to come and score a touch down on her at any moment.

'Handsome looking lot of girls you've got here,' says a voice. I turn round to see who it is, forgetting that I've undone my bikini top and see Ted giving me an old-fashioned look. I clutch my top to my breasts and lie down again smartly.

'Don't lie in the sun too long, girls,' says Ted. 'It'll burn the backsides off you. We're at seven thousand feet here. I just wanted to say that we leave to see the lions at 4.0 p.m., tell all the guests and make sure that if they are coming they are there on time.' He has an edge of authority to his voice, that reminds me of Hiram underneath the breezy exterior.

We go in covered landrovers to the tree house. They drive into an enclosure around the base of the tree house, the hunters shut the gates and we climb up to a platform. It is very simple but there is an Indian steward serving drinks and rugs and skins cover the floor. The sun begins to go down over the forest, and the carcase of a deer is dropped just below us. Immediately a huge lioness slinks out of the bushes, followed by three more. The sight of them stops me in mid gin and tonic. We are only fifteen or so feet above them. Only one lioness begins to tear at the carcase. Ted explains that there is a list of priority, strictly observed. Suddenly a huge roar tears the evening apart.

'Here it comes,' whispers Ted.

A male lion comes out of the bush. It is almost dark now in the tree house and Ted turns on a spotlight. The lion's yellow eyes look at it evilly and he roars again. The tree house trembles.

'That's crazy, man,' says Rip, 'I'm really into lions.'

Jens's two girls cling to him in terror. I clutch Ted's arm in fright, and he pats my shoulder sympathetically, as one might a child's.

'Don't worry, he's used to us by now.'

Flash guns pop, drinks flow and down below about eight lions in all tear the carcase apart as though it were corned beef.

Then off they go, roaring, into the night.

'Ted, that is just the most fantastic sight I have ever seen. I have done every goddam game reserve in Africa, and I have never seen a sight like it.'

We light some storm lanterns and have another sundowner, before getting back into the jeeps.

Norman is quite impressed by it all, too.

'I've been to the lion park at Woburn,' he says, 'but this is much better. Don't you think so, Madge.'

'Well at Woburn there's more of them.'

'Ah, true, but these 'ere are wild lions.'

'Yes, you're right there, Norman.'

Round the boma the stories fly thick and fast. A very shy young hunter called Peter is asked to tell his story of how he killed a lion with a sheath knife.

'Sounds interesting.'

83

'Not that sort of sheath, Kate.'

It is quite unbelievable, but as the flames from the fire die down and we sip brandies, Peter's quiet South African voice gets to us all.

'And then the great big bugger, excuse me ladies, leapt on me just as I was relieving myself behind a tree. I fell down, pulled out my knife and stuck it right in the jugular. Even as he was dying, the bastard made a great big hole in my side.'

'And he'll be happy to show it to you, free of charge, any time that's convenient to you, in the privacy of your own rondavel,' adds Ted.

It is an absolutely cloudless night. Crickets and other insects make a constant background to all conversation. Rip seems to be particularly sensitive to the atmosphere – I feel it may be a hopeful sign; if we can get him interested and a little happy, anything could happen. His large eyes are burning brighter than before and he has stopped shaking, though he is still drinking carrot juice.

Norman gets out his ukelele and sings *Ukelele Man*, which we all applaud roundly. In the midst of all this happiness I suddenly miss Rick desperately. He said he was coming out to Kenya soon, but I need him now.

'Missing him?' asks Kate, who knows me well.

'And you?'

'Yes, but there are so many lovely fellers here, even Bridget can't handle them all, so let's not be left at the start.'

I laugh.

'I wonder about old Ted there.'

'You will have to move fast. Amanda Greer is after him.'

Amanda's beautiful, expensive face is gazing at Ted adoringly. Her silk Pucci shirt is open to reveal her round, hand-made breasts, and she keeps licking her lips suggestively.

'God's gift to White Hunters, Ski Instructors and Gigolos,' says Pincher. 'She's been through the lot in every resort in the world. Whole goddam structure is going to fall apart one day, revealing a frail old lady inside, like Whistler's mother.

'How old is she?'

'About sixty.'

84

'Her last husband, owned every Greer's store in the world, one hundred percent.'

When I get to know her, I find her sweet and generous, but completely neurotic about her looks. She changes them like some people change their hair styles.

'Listen, honey, I can buy anything in the world, but I'm trying to buy beauty and youth, and that is not easy,' she tells me later.

'By the time she has left here one of these boys,' she gestures to the hunters, 'is gonna be richer than he ever dreamed of, all because of her. If she takes a shine to someone she gives him a huge gift before getting rid of him. I've warned them all.'

'Well, I just hope it's not Ted,' I say, without thinking, but Ted is man enough for the situation.

'Frank, come here,' he says. One of the hunters steps up. Take Miss Greer to the observation hut to see the hippos feeding. Miss Greer, we keep this walk specially for the most beautiful woman present,' he adds in a low voice, and she positively glows.

'Come on, Frankie boy, do what your uncle says.' And off they go.

No one wants to gamble. The place is so exciting, and out beyond the camp all sorts of jungle noises have started up, so it seems a waste to go indoors. We sit around the campfire for hours until it gets rather cold: then Jens invites us to his rondavel me, Ted, Kate, Lindy and Rip. The others have all gone to bed or about their business. We sit about and drink brandy for a while, then Jens proposes a game. It's called Truth.

'What happens is that everyone must say for ten seconds something he or she feels about the other members of dis group ja?'

It doesn't sound like a lot of fun to me, but I've had a hell of a lot to drink, so I'm game to try.

Chantal starts. In a charming accent, as though she were talking about vegetables, she says,

'I believe that Rip 'as got ze biggest coque in this room.'

'Dat's is very good, now your turn, Lindy.'

Lindy is terribly embarrassed, poor soul, even though she is not sober by any means.

'I would like to take all my clothes off and go for a swim.'

'That is not quite right, liebchen, but it is OK. Now you, Rip.'

'Man, I'm into girls with only one tit. I think Kate has only got one.'

We all laugh as Kate is bursting out of her safari suit in all directions. She opens it and pretends to have a peep.

'No, sorry, two.'

'Helga.'

'I would like to kiss Chantal.' She does so, fully and explicitly. We watch, fascinated. Jens gets quite animated.

'And you, Penny.'

'I would like to make love to the most exciting man here.'

'OK, very clever; now you Ted.'

'I would like to make love to the girl who sunbathes without her top.' As he says it, he looks at Jens, but I know who he means, clever old me.

Jens says he wants to kiss Kate, which he does. Ted kisses me, the two girls begin to kiss each other on the other bed, and Lindy and Rip go off down the path, the frail Rip supporting Lindy who is stumbling. Kate and Jens lie on the other bed together, so I take Ted's hand and we leave.

There are no preliminaries. We go straight to his bungalow. We don't need to say a word. The sight of the two fallen angels clasping each other on the bed, their purple mouths glued together, has done away with any need for pretence.

He lifts me on to the bed, takes off my safari suit and holds my breasts in his hands.

'Lovely, beautiful.'

He undresses quickly and we're lying in the moonlight on a thick fur while we feel each other's bodies. I feel incredibly aroused, and I can feel that he is too. I want so much to have him inside me. His fingers reach under my panties and begin to stroke me. I come once before he has even entered me, and then I take off my panties and lie back. For a moment he just looks at me.

'You're lovely.'

'So are you, Ted. Ted whatever your name is.'

And I draw him on top of me. He makes love like a sailor in a brothel, but it suits my mood. He is violent and yet not unthoughtful; I begin to scream with pleasure and pain and I am glad that Kate is not there to hear me. Ted is like a

86

raging torrent; when it slackens we lie back bruised, our bodies wet despite the air-conditioning.

'Welcome to Africa, darling.'

'I think I am going to like it here.' I say, stroking him lightly. To my amazement he seems to be becoming aroused again. It must be something in the water in these parts.

As dawn is breaking, I practically crawl back to our rondavel. To be more accurate, I do a sort of scuttle, like a shagged-out crab.

CHAPTER 11

Kate and I compare notes in the morning, as we prepare to get out on the morning game-spotting run. It is a beautiful morning, the sun already up, and down by the river we can see various antelope grazing peacefully.

'Why don't we just lie in bed and do our game-spotting from here,' I suggest.

'And get Ted, the demon lover over at regular intervals.'

'Tell me about you and Jens and those little lesbians.'

'I don't think they are lesbians, actually. They certainly joined in the fun. Do you know, that Helga is only sixteen?'

'My God, Kate, what went on?'

Even for Kate, this seems a bit exotic. Three girls and one man. I can't believe it.

'Were they there all the time.'

'I know this will sound silly, but Jens said quite openly that he isn't turned on unless someone is watching him. That's why he keeps two girls, so there's always an audience. You may think it's kinky, but when you've been around as much as Jens, it makes sense. Anyway, I was so stoned with all that brandy the whole thing seemed like a very good romp to me.'

I am a little shocked, in a funny way. I know I'm not the most chaste girl in the world, but sex seems to me to be something between two people, not a sort of party game for all participants.

'Jens said that if you ever wanted to join in he would be delighted to have you along.' This is very selfless of our Kate. Still if you're already sharing your man with two others, why not three others. It keeps it friendly.

Ted appears at our door, his face bright, brown and outdoorsy. He gives me a kiss and says,

'Hurry up, girls, the jeeps are leaving in five minutes. I won't be coming, but you should go out and get used to it for the first few mornings.'

Dear Ted, he's so capable, and I don't just mean in bed. But I must say, I have a slight feeling of regret about having got involved with him. For one Rick and Jim are going to turn up one day soon, and for two he suddenly seems a little schoolmasterish with his pipe and the way he bustles about.

The five jeeps set off on their runs, each one loaded with guns, drinks, binoculars and a game spotter, who sits on a high seat at the back. One hunter drives each jeep and they keep in touch by radio.

I go with Frank, and Amanda Greer's lot. Amanda and I sit together. She is dying to tell me about Frank.

'Absolutely marvellous lover, that boy. It must be all the red meat they eat around here. Get way, goddam insects, as I was saying, marvellous lover. I think I am going to enjoy it here more than all the other game parks I've been to. Mind you, you can't really beat a safari. Nossir, your own hunters, your own tents and off you go. But damned uncomfortable, and you can't really ball in a camp bed, I can tell you. At Nyanda I damn near broke my coccyx when a camp bed collapsed, bringing me and Jimmy, no Basil, damned silly name that, crashing to the ground.'

I am trying to look at the game, but she isn't much interested.

'Don't worry about those little brown deer, Tommys we call them, those little mothers are everywhere. Really all these animals are just cows dressed up in fancy dress.'

As she says this, a huge giraffe appears in the track. Frank slows the jeep and we drive to within a few yards of it before it lopes off, as though in slow motion, into the undergrowth. It is the biggest thing I have ever seen in my life and so beautiful it takes the breath away. But my mood is quickly shattered.

'It's a bull,' says Frank.

'Jesus, it's got even bigger balls that my second husband,' says Amanda, which has the whole jeep in hysterics.

'I think we'll go over to the hippo pool and see if there are any calves about,' suggests Frank, 'if you people agree.'

On the way we see all manner of game, even a cheetah which Amanda finds exciting, because she's only seen six before, very rare they are, and I am beginning to distinguish between a Thompson's gazelle and a wildebeest, of which there are also thousands. Ugly things with vicious looking horns, but, so Frank tells us, very gentle dispositions, which I find comforting because I am sure a whole herd of them if they made up their mind to indulge in some collective action, could make a nasty mess of a jeep full of millionaires. At the hippo pool, we are told we can get out, but not to go too close to the edge and to be sure not to make a noise as hippos are easily irritated.

At first I can't see a thing, just an expanse of greeny grey water, then suddenly there's a blowing and snorting and huge heads appear out of the water.

'There's a calf,' says Frank, 'look sitting on its mother's back.'

Its the dearest little thing, though actually rather bigger than your average Shetland pony, but compared with the fully grown hippos it looks positively petite. Frank now looks pleased, and he gets on the radio to other jeeps to spread the news of the nativity. At this point the hippos begin to set sail in our direction, about ten big heads, with huge mouths opening and roaring, I run like hell for the jeep, but they only come to within five yards of the bank before calling a truce.

'Very aggressive animals,' says Frank, 'if you ever get between them and water when they're out grazing, you're dead.'

Grazing! They look to me as though they eat a herd of Thompson's gazelles each day.

By the time we get back to camp, we're all experienced game spotters with stories to tell each other. Amanda has invited me to her bungalow for a drink after breakfast which I turn down on account of pressure of work. Breakfast, it's still only eight o'clock, is much appreciated. They've even got Loch Fyne kippers, says the Indian steward, who is charming. Kate and I have two each. Norman and Madge have four each and some All Bran, and all the Americans look at us as though we had lost our marbles. Jens and his two girls, all three arm-in-arm appear, and sit down. They seem to be hungry, but it's not from game-spotting as they haven't done any of that.

After breakfast we have a few small things to do, but really our tasks are so undemanding that I feel a bit foolish. Pincher explains that Mr Firefly always thinks pretty and efficient girls keep an enterprise happy, and anyway, things will liven up. Bridget seems to be doing Pincher a lot of good, because he only gives me one tiny tweak in the whole of our conversation, or 'briefing' as he likes to call it. Even he's looking healthy. I spend the rest of the morning by the pool with Kate and one or two of the other girls. We chat to the guests. I am becoming particularly fond of Norman Birtwhistle, who appears in a huge pair of trunks and swims energetically, with one foot on the ground. Madge unwraps herself from a giant beach wrap, and lies in the sun, surrounded by insect repellents and suncream bottles. The more energetic have gone out for walks with trackers, but I don't fancy that in this heat.

I fall into conversation with Frank, the hunter. He is really quite chuffed about his conquest, and wants to talk to someone, and for some reason, he thinks of me as a sister, which I consider a little premature, I mean that's a stage you usually reach after all the other has ebbed away.

'Do you know she used to be a top model,' he says. I hate to disillusion him by telling how many years and facelifts ago that was.

'Yes, she's invited me to her house in the Bahamas during the close season.'

'Don't you like living out here?'

'I love it, but you know it's like any other job, a change is good for you from time to time.'

'They say she's very rich,' I add, a little maliciously.

'Yes, but she's so beautiful, I mean she knows all the most famous people in the world.'

Poor Frank. With his sincere, handsome face and square, muscular body he is very attractive. But Amanda will chew him up and spit him out in little pieces before he knows what day it is.

As she said to me in the jeep, you can't take these ski instructors or white hunters home. Like Italian wines, they don't travel. Fortunately Norman breaks up our discussion.

'We saw an elephant,' he says triumphantly. 'Wait till I show them my pictures at the club when I get back. If the buggers come out. I've never 'ad a camera before, but Perlmutter is going to give me his Nikon, so he says. He's got four, so he won't miss it. Come on Madge, show us your cleavage, lass, give us a big smile.' Click. Click. Crafty old Norm manages to get a few shots of my cleavage as well, and I actually incite him by leaning forward and drawing my shoulders together. He likes it, and who am I to deny him such a simple pleasure.

We seem to start drinking very early out here, but then we have been up since five. Pimms is my favourite drink for a hot day, and I introduce Norman and Madge to it, as well as the Perlmutters. Perlmutter looks a bit like a walking camera shop when he comes back, telephoto lenses, Nikons, and a cartridge belt full of film.

Pincher tells me that Mr Firefly, Jim and Rick are coming over the next day, to see how we're getting on.

'So make sure all your girls are looking presentable when he arrives.'

'I'm a bit worried about Bridget, Mr Dobermann, I think she's looking a little strained.'

'Bitch,' he says, but he smiles at the same time. You've got to hand it to old Pincher, he's got a bit of style. The girl in question is out on a ramble with one of the hunters, a tall black man, who is going to show her a family of warthogs, which Bridget thinks are cute.

'Old Mbuna will probably show her his black mamba,' says Ted. 'That lad is famous in these parts, for his parts!'

'And what about you Ted? Are you famous in these parts?'

'I don't do too badly, for a country boy.'

'No you don't,' I say, giving him a kiss.

'After lunch we usually have a siesta in the heat of the day, so pop round to my bungalow.

'What sort of an example is this for the other staff,' but I know I will and he knows I will. The only cloud on my horizon is the fact that Rick is due some time tomorrow. What am I going to tell Ted? I try to get some help from Kate, but all she says is,

'Say you've got the clap.'

'I don't know what's come over you, Kate.'

At lunch I put the problem to Amanda, who is one of those girls you can immediately confide your deepest secrets to.

'Listen, honey, I'll think of something. You've still got until tomorrow, so don't fret. Your Auntie Mandy will think of something.'

She makes me feel much better, but I am a little worried about what she's come up with. Kate isn't the least bit worried about her little scene with Jens.

'He won't mind. He'll just keep quiet until Jim's gone. You see how much easier it is not to get involved.'

I know that deep down Kate has been missing Jim as much as I have been missing Rick, but she doesn't believe in letting the grass grow under her feet, or bottom for that matter. And she's right in a way. Because, as I discover after lunch, Ted is becoming very fond of me. I like him a lot too, and although we don't quite recapture the excitement of last night, we make love leisurely and deeply in the darkened bungalow. I fall asleep in his arms, and he kisses me tenderly. When I wake up he's gone. I've got all my girls together for a four o'clock briefing, and it's already five to. I leap into my clothes as fast as I can and race over to our bungalow, very conscious that I've left my bra behind as I run.

'Get between a hippo and the water, did you dear,' says Kate.

'Oh shut up. I don't think you're taking your responsibilities in the right spirit.'

There's a knock on the door. The girls have arrived.

'Talk to them while I have a wash.'

Kate lets them in and I try to straighten myself up in the bathroom. Pimms, hot sun and midday love-making have left their mark. Looking like something that's just crawled out of a haystack, I go back into the room.

Kate says:

'And now the star of our show, to talk to you about deportment, make-up, and general tidiness, Chief Stewardess Penelope Sutton.'

Bloody Kate. Still, it breaks down any barriers there might have been.

'What Kate and I have to tell you is that Mr Firefly is coming tomorrow, and Mr Dobermann wants all to look cool and organized. Try and make some notes about the guests, what their comments are, in private, to you. Also any improvements to the programme. We don't want to look as though we've just spent our first few days in riotous living.'

'No we don't,' says Bridget, eyes shining, 'Mr Firefly is such a demanding man!' She sounds like the leader of a brownie troupe, this little raver. The odd thing is she means it.

Lindy has a problem.

'What shall we do about Rip? I mean he is losing his mind fast, but he won't go to a doctor. I really think he should go back to hospital. Either that or be given some heroin. I can't bear to see him suffer.'

'Well, I think this is right outside our authority. Mr Dobermann must get the doctor to see him. You tell Mr Dobermann the whole story.'

After the other girls have gone, Lindy tells us the whole story. Rip has been vomiting blood, has eaten nothing but carrot juice, and is suffering from hallucinations. But he won't let Lindy fetch a doctor, and he doesn't want her to leave his sight for a moment. I remember my horrifying experience on the plane the other night like a vivid nightmare, so I sympathize with Lindy. We must get a doctor to see him. Dobermann gets on the radio, and within two hours a light plane is taxiing up the runway. As we come back from the lion feeding, we see Rip being taken away on a stretcher, Lindy clutching his hand and sobbing. He is dead.

It is a terrible shock. Particularly as I was cradling him in my arms so recently, although it seems like ages ago.

Dobermann is reassuring.

'We knew he was very ill. But it was a chance. Mr Firefly personally authorized this trip. Now we have to get back to work. None of the other guests must know that he died of drug addiction, and nobody is to talk to any reporters, because I am sure a few will try and find their way out here. Now, honey, this is where you start to earn your wage.'

And earn it we do. Lindy is put to bed under sedation, we circulate among the guests explaining that Rip has died, after a long illness. It's not too difficult, really, because none of the guests had ever spoken to the dark, hunched-up figure behind the dark glasses. Really only Jens had ever heard him utter a word.

'Chinese heroin,' says Jens. 'Dis stuff is murder. Poor boy.'

I don't try to pretend anything else to Jens. He knows, sees, feels everything. Kate is marvellous, of course. You need someone like her in a crisis. By midnight, the pale, thin corpse is forgotten by everyone except Lindy. The bright African moonlight looks cold and deadly to me tonight. I am glad Rick is coming in the morning.

As I slip off to bed when the last of the guests have finished gambling, Ted catches hold of my arm.

'Darling, while Rick is here, I won't be able to see you, OK?'

'I understand Ted,' I say, but never have I understood anything less clearly in my life. Kate and I try to puzzle it out in bed, but the solution does not come. Poor Lindy comes over to our bungalow, braving the dark in her misery. We tuck her up in Kate's bed and Kate hops in with me. I begin to understand why Kate has so many lovers – she's a very comfy sleeper.

CHAPTER 12

A gleaming Lear jet makes a pass over the camp just before lunch. I find my heart giving a little leap. It's Hiram's special private, personalized plane, piloted by his special, personalized pilot. Kate and I jump into a jeep and race out to the airstrip. For such a remote part of nowhere, it's getting pretty crowded with aircraft. When Rick makes a perfect landing, there are three Lear jets and two other light planes, as well as the cargo plane. It seems to take ages for Rick to park it right in line with the other planes. Hiram appears down the stairs first, followed by Jim, who is carrying three briefcases, looking a bit like a missionary in search of a tribe to convert, what with his striped linen suit. At last Rick comes down the stairs, and despite everything I run and hurl myself into his arms. He is a bit embarrassed in front of his boss, but Hiram just smiles.

'How are you girls?' he asks. 'Terrible business about Rip Mathews, but it was better for him to die out here than in a ghastly hospital for addicts. Now we must put all that behind us. How's it been going?'

His arrival seems to clear the air. Rick, too, is very comforting and worried about us all.

'Listen boys,' says Hiram, 'You all take the day off and relax, OK?'

What could be better news? Most of the guests have gone on a fishing and barbecue trip to a smaller camp miles away and aren't expected back till nightfall, so we've little enough to do.

Rick goes back to the plane and comes striding back with a parcel.

'Little something I picked up for you in Europe.'

'Oh, Rick, what is it.'

'Don't open it now, honey, wait till we get inside. Oh I sure have missed you. Those German girls just aren't the same.'

Kate and Jim have disappeared with Hiram and his driver, so we drive down to the camp with Mbuna. He knows Rick of old, and, like everybody who comes into contact with him, is delighted to see him back. He promises to take us that afternoon to see something special he's not told anyone about.

When we get inside, I say, 'What's this about German girls?'

'Just kidding. What you been up to? Any of these wild hunter fellers?'

'Rick, how can you say such a thing?'

'Let's put it this way, if I was one of them I wouldn't let something like you lie about here unmolested.'

And he starts to molest. Old Rick is one of the speediest undressers I have ever met. In a moment we're both naked, clothes thrown about the room as if we only had a few moments of life. In fact, with Rick I always have the feeling that he is going to be off again in a plane at any moment, so I try to make the best of it. I know how much he likes it, so my lips slide down his body, until I feel him warm and firm. But we are so excited that he is soon on top of me and in me without any preparation at all, and I am ready for him. We make love frantically and I am sobbing with happiness.

'I told you I always cry when I am happy.'

'You are one crazy kid, but I love you.'

'Oh, Rick, I've missed you something rotten.'

'Aren't you going to see what I brought you?' I leap off the bed and grab the parcel. The wrapping says 'Boucheron Place Vendome, Paris'. Even I know that Boucheron is one of the world's most exclusive jewellery shops. In a tiny velvet-lined box is a diamond pendant.

'I want you to wear it and think of me when I'm not here.'

'You shouldn't have. Oh, my God, it's beautiful.'

'Here, let me put it on, as they say in the movies. You look beautiful. Do you know I've never made it with a woman wearing only a diamond before,' says he as he eases me back on to the bed.

For ten minutes the diamond is driven right out of my mind. We lie back, me with a spectacular bikini mark after my sunbathing, with just this one, large, almost obscene diamond resting between my breasts. And Rick, so lean and muscular, next to me smiling to himself. People who like to give presents are my sort of people, I find, and not for the obvious reason either. But I've never had a present like this before. I feel so low about my fling with Ted and I almost want to confess and let Rick know that I was missing him all the time. Of course I don't, but it's the thought that counts, they say.

'Come on, baby, we got a lot to do,' says Rick as he pulls on his clothes. He looks his best in outdoor wear, and he's got the most beautiful guerilla camouflage jacket and trousers, with a soft hat – the sort of thing no guerilla would ever be able to afford in a million years, but it looks smashing. We collect Mbuna, and try to get his secret out of him, but he just drives the jeep with a smile on his polished face. Everyone seems to be smiling today. Rick loves Africa in the same way he loves the Firefly Ranch, with an intense passion. He knows all the animals, and not just the big ones but the birds, rodents and insects too.

'Well, Mbuna you old bastard, what have you got for us?'

But he's not telling. After a lot of stopping the jeep and looking at tracks, he motions us to follow, quietly, and we get out. I am terrified. One of those lions could be anywhere, and the way they rip up a gazelle doesn't leave much hope for me. Mbuna hasn't even got a gun with him. It's like a Sunday stroll in Hyde Park as far as these two are concerned. Mbuna is looking intently at the ground as we make our way slowly through some dense scrub. I am looking intently for a large tree to climb, but there aren't any – for the first time in weeks. I wish I were back in London, preferably in a pub with a large gin and tonic in my hand. But the intrepid explorers press on, and I am certainly not going to be left behind, so I cling to Rick's hand. Mbuna whispers something to Rick and he points. It looks like the side of a house to me, but Rick says,

'White rhino.'

And we're only twenty yards away!

'Goddam, we've done it, we've done it,' Rick suddenly shouts, and hugs Mbuna. The rhino instantly begins to charge, like half a housing estate on the hoof. Rick seizes me, and shuts me up. We stand like pillars, and the rhino stops fifteen yards off, pawing the ground. It's then that I see the baby white rhino. It is a miniaturized version of its mum, so small and frail by comparison, trotting around like a confused child.

We back off to a safe distance, or what these maniacs consider a safe distance, and Rick explains.

'I personally flew that old cow and her mate from South Africa. The first white rhinos in these parts, and look, they've bred. Isn't she beautiful? Mbuna, you're a genius.'

Beautiful it isn't, but it certainly is an impressive animal, and the little baby is too sweet for words.

'I don't tell anybody, Rick, I follow the cow for weeks and I know she pregnant, then yesterday I see the calf. One day old.'

Rick gets his long lens going and takes literally hundreds of pictures of the happy event.

'Mr Firefly sure is going to be glad about this. Hell, that animal and its mate almost destoyed one of our planes when the tranquilizer wore off, and it was my idea to import some of them to Mula Mula. Come on baby let's leave them in peace and go get a big drink.'

I am only too happy to get back to the jeep. Rick explains that white rhino are extinct in these parts and this is the first successful attempt to breed them. They are much tamer than their black cousins and very very short-sighted. All you do is stand still and they'll leave you alone. The man says. Though not the black ones, they love a good charge even though they can't see much better. Rick is so happy, I catch his mood instantly. How he cares about things! I know that I could become interested in wild life and conservation with his enthusiasm and knowledge to guide me.

Hiram is delighted by the news, but I suspect he's delighted because Rick has been successful.

'That goddam baby rhino cost me nearly twenty-five thousand dollars to produce. We had to buy a pair in South Africa, fly them up here, watch them for days, and then repair the plane, or what was left of it. Still, if I hadn't done it, this boy would have resigned, wouldn't you?'

'Sure would have, Mr Firefly?'

'You are a blackmailer, son, that's what you are. Now make the most of your day off, because it's back to work tomorrow. I want to go to Nairobi and fetch Barbra-Ann, as well as do some business with the government.'

Rick does not keep still for a moment. We have a hurried lunch and set off again, this time to see some lions. I am pleased to see that Mbuna has his gun with him. Jim and

Kate come too, though Jim seems much more interested in Kate than the wild life. In fact they're so intent on each other that they miss the quick glimpse we get of an elephant. Kate is looking so healthy and sexy, in a safari suit with the top three buttons undone, and lots of golden brown chest popping out, who can blame Jim? Certainly not Rick and I. But the sight of a pride of lions, resting peacefully in the shade of some thorn trees, three females and two huge males, stirs us all up. One of the males gets up, its tail twitching, and growls. Mbuna only backs the jeep closer. In this vast wilderness they seem to know every animal.

'Old Roger is looking a bit pissed-off today.'

'Him getting old. Like old man with no more girlfriend.'

When they growl, the earth seems to shake.

'Aren't we a bit close, Rick?'

Rick doesn't think so, but I notice Mbuna has the engine running and has cocked his gun. Mbuna expects some cubs soon, so that's maybe why the lions are getting a bit edgy.

'I'm getting a bit edgy myself,' says Kate. The second lion gets up and begins to growl, and Mbuna eases the jeep away.

'Him very bad, that one. Very bad,' says Mbuna.

'They're just like people. You get to know their characters. Old Roger there, he's been on the reserve for years, and you could practically pull his tail, but some of the other lions move in and out of Mula Mula and you have no idea of what sort of company they've been mixing in.'

As the sun goes down over the river, Rick, Jim, Kate and I sit with Mbuna and talk animals and adventures. Mbuna used to be a regular hunter, taking Americans and others on safari for a safari firm, but big game hunting has suffered recently. More people are interested in conservation, and Mbuna tells us that he became converted to it, despite having been brought up to hunt and trained as a 'White Hunter'.

'Blackest white hunter you ever saw,' says Rick, with a laugh. When Mbuna laughs he makes quite a performance of it. His enormous hands slap his thighs and tears start in his eyes. He is incredibly handsome, so lithe and graceful, it wouldn't surprise me at all if Pincher is right and he is the local Romeo.

In Hiram's honour, a special banquet has been prepared. Suckling pig is being roasted on the fire and the smells waft all over the camp. The guests come back from their various trips ravenous and thirsty. It is amazing the effect the place is having on them. Even Jens's two girls are looking healthy and innocent; that pale, slightly depraved look has gone. They are full of what they have seen and done and are giggling like kids. Which they are, really, kids playing at being actresses, kids dressed up for Jens's world. Jens, though has a certain magnetism. He is so worldly, yet understanding with it. He and Rick get on like a house on fire, particularly as Rick can name most of his movies. Soon we have quite a party going; Hiram is chatting to all the guests, the champagne and fresh orange juice cocktails are disappearing at an alarming rate. Madge Birtwhistle, a piece of sticking plaster over her nose, has acquired a great taste for dry Martinis, while Norman is trying to teach Chantal to do the Hokey Cokey. It seems to involve a great deal of pushing and prodding to get her to do it right, but Norm gets away with it.

Dinner is out of this world. We sit in the boma and the cooks carve the suckling pigs in front of our eyes. Bridget isn't sure she's going to have any after seeing the whole family running around with their little tails in the air, but she succumbs. Even Lindy cheers up under the influence of such a beautiful evening.

Only one thing mars my happiness slightly. Ted. He has been very withdrawn, and is now with Amanda, talking quietly, without joining in the general hilarity. What has she done to him? Surprisingly, in the circumstances, I feel a little jealousy – the way the two of them are sitting so intimately together, and yet she has saved me from a terrible problem. The two of them get up and leave the boma.

'Thinking about something?' asks Rick.

'Just you, darling,' I lie.

'We're bringing a photographer and writer out from Nairobi tomorrow. To cover the trip and help with the publicity. Not that we need any more, but the whole venture seems to have caught alight. Every socialite in the world is booked for the next two flights.'

'Who's the photographer?' I ask without really wanting to hear the answer.

'Richard somebody, a British photographer. You may know him.'

'London is a very big place,' I say.

Richard. I could believe anything of him, but this is incredible. How did he worm his way into an assignment like this? Of course he does know Hiram slightly, or someone in the organization.

'Richard? Christ you really are in a mess now.' Kate at her most helpful. 'What are you going to do?'

'Kate, I don't know. Still, Richard isn't the sort to care. But Rick must not find out.'

'You'll just have to explain it all to Richard as soon as he arrives and hope he can keep quiet.'

'You know him. He'll use it in some way.'

'What if he starts talking to Rick on the way from Nairobi?'

The whole thing is crashing down about my ears. It's so unfair. Kate doesn't help much by muttering something about the wages of sin.

'Look who's bloody talking. What if Richard shoots his mouth off to Rick, and Rick tells Jim. Then where are you?'

'Up a bloody gum tree,' she says laughing, 'don't worry, Penny, it'll all be OK.' But she doesn't sound too convinced.

Rick sets off for Nairobi in the morning and Kate and I go about our tasks a little anxiously. At least Ted has hardly said a word to me since I told Amanda my problems. Jim and Kate go off happily for a swim, and I feel so miserable, I go to see Amanda.

'What's the matter honey? Your dream lover's coming back, isn't he?'

'Amanda what did you say to Ted?'

'It wasn't difficult, darling. I told him Rick was mad about you, and to keep in with Firefly you would have to be nice to him while he was here. Anyway, I also told him a few more tiny white lies. Poor boy was almost inconsolable. But I found a way of consoling him, I sure did.'

'Amanda, you're terrible. You didn't go to bed with him, did you?'

'No mostly on the rug in the bathroom. It was cooler in there.'

I am almost speechless.

'Well I did it for you, darling. I mean I had to do something to get his mind off you. While we were leapfrogging around the bathroom, you were never out of my thoughts for a moment.'

'What about Frank?'

'Oh poor boy. So boring. Always wanting to turn the light out and tell me hunting stories. I think he's in love with me. What would I do with a tame white hunter? He could shoot the rats in the barn, I suppose.'

Poor Frank. I can't help laughing, though she is cruel. Selfish people can be quite charming, probably because they don't care about the normal considerations.

'Anyway, I've given him a pair of guns to be made at Purdey's in London. He thinks that's just fantastic. They won't be ready for two years, by which time there will be nothing left to shoot anyway.'

Norman corners me and tries to get me to come to his bungalow for a drink, but my heart is not in it.

CHAPTER 13

'I believe this gentleman is a friend of yours.'

'What's the matter, Rick?'

But he doesn't reply to my question. Richard jumps out of the jeep and gives me a big kiss. But Rick has simply walked off.

'You didn't tell him, did you?'

'Tell him what?'

'You know what I mean.'

'Well, how was I to know you and that big hunk of corn-bread had shacked up. Aren't you pleased to see me.'

'You are a bastard and I wish to god I had never, ever met you.'

'Darling, remember who introduced you to this set-up. Now I am here to do an exlusive photo story for *Sprinkel*.'

'Jesus, Richard, I have got very fond of Rick and now you've gone and screwed it all up.'

'What about me? I thought you were fond of me.'

'Yes, but you know what I mean.'

'Look, darling, I am here to do a story and then you won't see me for dust, and you and muscles can kiss and make up. How's your friend with the big tits?'

In point of fact, Kate is in tears. Jim has told her that he is leaving the next morning, and anyway he doesn't care to see her again. How news travels in these parts. I get a little aggressive myself about this sort of old-fashioned masculine behaviour. Jim and Rick are going around as though there is a bad smell not a million miles from the end of their noses. So when Rick comes to me and says,

'Penny, I really couldn't believe what that fink told me. How could you do this to me?'

I say, 'Why don't you and Jim piss off back to Albuquerque where you belong with those cowgirls.'

In my heart I am trying to say something totally different, but his self-righteous look irritates me.

'We are all off tomorrow anyway, so I guess that's the end

of that.' He turns and goes, so tall and strong. I want to run after him and throw my arms around him, and tell him how much I care for him and his white rhino and all those silly things. But I cannot.

Richard settles in fast. By the end of dinner he has met everybody, charmed the panties off all the girls, who think his accent is just cute, and even made me smile once or twice. Jim and Rick sit as far from us as they can, and Amanda and Ted have gone off for a jaunt to Ngorogoro. Richard and Hiram become engaged in a deep conversation. He has such a nerve, nobody can resist him. He has obviously done his homework, because he knows everyone here and what they are worth. As he explains it to me, about as much as the gold reserves of Ireland, which sounds impressive.

'Tell me about Rip Mathews, the songwriter and pop legend?'

'I don't know much about him.'

'Well, what was he like?'

'Very quiet. Mr Firefly says he has been ill for a long time.'

'Junk. He was a junkie. Everybody knew he was a main-liner.'

'That's not what we heard.'

'Well you heard wrong.'

'Ask Mr Firefly.'

'I have.'

'What did he say.'

'A mystery illness, not unlike leukaemia.'

'Well there you are then. I wouldn't know.'

'Look, I don't care about that. I know, the world knows he died of dope. I have already seen his doctor on the way here. What I want is an exclusive story. Did anybody particularly get to know him?'

'Only Lindy. She talked to him a bit before he died.'

'Lindy, with the long legs. OK, I'll talk to her.'

As smooth as treacle he whisks Lindy off for a dance leaving me and Kate, like the maiden aunts at a twenty-first party. Norman puts an arm around Kate, running a hand over one of her boobs in the process, but he's such a lovely fellow you can't really hold it against him. Although he's all for holding his against you.

'What 'appened to your friends? They look a bit bloody snooty to me tonight.'

'They've gone off us.'

'Don't worry about it, lass, all these Americans are Mother's Boys. Do you know, during the war one of those buggers came to stay with us and all he would bloody drink was bloody coke. I ask yer, no wonder they couldn't beat those little fellers in Vietnam. I shouldn't wonder if they're missing their mams.'

He gives us both a big hug, which he really means to cheer us up. He's not a big man, Norm, and he almost disappears between Kate's boobs, which makes me laugh.

'Come out, number nine, your times up lad,' says Kate.

'Norman Birtwhistle, what are you doing?' says Madge.

'Nowt much, Madge. Nowt as would interest you, no-how.' Kate and I are getting disastrously drunk, though in this company you have to practically drop down dead to be noticed.

'Let's go and talk to Jens.'

'OK, but I'm not having any talk about foursomes, or fivesomes.'

Jens is telling a story about a well-known film star who is bisexual. The way he tells it, you would think being bisexual was a bit like having an equity card in Hollywood – almost essential if you want to get on. Chantal and Helga, wearing matching, clinging long satin dresses, slit almost to the crotch, each have a hand on his shoulder. They're still eating, their little sharp teeth tearing into a chop each. Jens loves an audience, in more ways than one, so when we join him he is delighted.

'Move your bumbi, Chantal, let Penny sit here. Anyway, then the director said to him: "OK, baby, if you don't get the lines this time, then just make your lips move and we'll dub it late." So dis actor says, "Listen sugar, if you'd kept your lips to themselves last night, I might be able to remember my lines this morning.' In front of a crew of sixty-five. I laughed so much I fell off my horse and broke my arm. Shooting delayed six days. Funny, yes?"

A silvery blonde lady of about fifty is gazing deeply into his eyes. She is the wife of a Florida property developer, and has seen all Jens's films since she was a little girl. Jens takes her hand and lays it on his thigh.

'Some of the finest actors, actresses and directors in the world haven't managed to get their hands that close to my heart,' he says. Somehow, whatever Jens says is acceptable. So when he puts an arm around me and says to the company, 'Excuse us, I must talk with Penelope.' I go with him.

I am terrified of snakes and things, but Jens seems hardly aware that there is any danger. We walk down to the swimming pool. A couple of animals start up in the dark and canter away. I grab Jens's arm.

'Don't worry. Any animals you hear won't worry you. It's the quiet ones that get you in the end. Tell me what happened to you and Kate with those American boys? Is it something to do with that photographer?'

I tell him the whole story. It's such a relief, and anyway I'm drunk. And as Kate says, he is so understanding. You know that nothing can shock him.

'What a silly story. Is dat all the matter is? Well, then that's their hard times, ja?'

I feel better about the whole thing. I give him a kiss, and he runs his hands over my breasts as he kisses me back but he does it in the way a horse breeder might feel a horse's legs.

'Well, let's celebrate. We'll get that Richard over and go to my cabin later. Good?'

'Good.'

A strange sight greets us on return to the fireside. Helga is asleep with her head in Kate's lap, and Chantal is trying to teach Norman how to do the latest Paris dance, which he is attempting with his trousers rolled up to his knees, for some reason known only to himself.

Pincher appears. 'Where's your photographer friend?'

'I don't know.'

'Well, I last saw him with Bridget.'

'Don't worry, Pincher old boy, he's probably just pumping her, for information, I mean,' says Jens. Pincher leaves in disarray.

'Bring some schnapps,' says Jens.

The fiery stuff practically takes my head off. We drink straight from the same bottle. The party becomes more and more riotous until Jens suggest we all go for a swim. I am more likely to drown than swim, but off we go.

Richard and Bridget emerge from the changing hut when they hear us coming.

'Hello!' says Richard, 'I thought you would never get here.' He is absolutely naked, but he strolls calmly over to the pool, before diving in. After a moment, Bridget throws away her towel and dives in too. Soon there is a mass of bodies, gleaming silvery in the water. Jens invents a game called, 'Touch the pubes', which he says is an adult form of tig. 'And I'm it.' He proves it immediately by giving me a sharp prod in the nether regions under water. I swim after Norman, who is dog-paddling as fast as he can, and give him a tug.

'Help, a shark got me.'

He chases after Helga, who swims like a slippery eel, but eventually he corners her.'

'Ja. Thank you you got me. You can go now.'

She swims after Richard, who is no match for her. He gets Chantal and so we go on until we are exhausted. The water is so warm it's like a bath. Thank the Lord Hiram is off with Barbra-Ann, at least I hope he is because four of his staff are floating around completely naked. Personal service is one thing, but this is ridiculous. Richard reappears, clothed.

'I just want to take a few pictures,' he says, but everyone threatens to murder him if he does.

We go off to Jens's bungalow. Not poor Norman, however; Madge seizes him. He manages to kiss us all goodbye, but she is quite firm.

'I've never been to an orgy,' he is heard muttering.

Bridget has to go off to Pincher, so it only leaves Richard, Jens, Kate the two girls and me, because Lindy has passed out.

'Don't leave her there, something will eat her.'

We carry her back to our bungalow. She is sick all over the bed, before falling asleep with an angelic smile on her face. We leave her. When we get to Jens's Helga and Chantal are both absolutely naked on one bed, their slim, girlish bodies entwined together like two snakes. It's amazing how unselfconscious they are.

'Come here,' they beckon to Richard, but he just smiles and watches. The four of us sit on the other bed as the two girls make love to each other. I can't believe that I am sitting here, watching two girls who could still be in school writhing on a bed.

'Pretty, ja?' says Jens, and he's right. They have obviously been told many times that they are beautiful and accept it as their right. They kiss each other all over, they stroke their slim legs and small round breasts, now one, now the other on top. My head begins to swim. I draw deeply on the schnapps. On the bed, the girls are beginning to get more urgent. They call to each other in French and German. Suddenly Richard is there between them. I am desperately jealous, but Jens pulls me to him and slips a hand into my blouse. Kate is already undoing her smock. I begin to understand how Kate felt the other night. With Jens around, anything seems possible, anything seems natural.

The three of us fall back on the bed. I reach for Jens and find Kate's hand already there, which makes us giggle. Soon all is confusion and passion. I find myself in bed with Richard and one of the girls, in the half-light I am not sure which one it is, but she is helping Richard as he eases himself on top of me. Her little hands caress my breasts as Richard enters me.

'Oh Richard, Oh Richard, yes, yes.'

Even as we make love, Helga, or Chantal kisses me. Her tongue slides into my mouth, and one of her legs becomes entangled with ours. Before I know what has happened, Jens is there, or is it Chantal, or even Kate, who knows? I seem to be asleep before it's all over, or perhaps I am dreaming all along. I fall asleep with the mocking, handsome, smile of Jens before my eyes.

At first light I try to get up, leaving the bodies like the aftermath of an air-crash. I have to disengage Helga, who is asleep with one of her legs between mine. She rolls over and slips an arm over Richard; even with my head pounding, I think how beautiful they look lying like that, a sheet up to their waists. I wake Kate, who feels as bad as I do.

We shower in cold water, and try to clean up the mess in our bungalow. Lindy is lying as we left her, wearing only a bra and her skirt. What would happen if Mr Firefly found us in this state? Somehow we get Lindy packed off to her room. Down by the river some elephants are feeding.

'I've often heard of people seeing elephants when they are drunk, but this is absurd,' says Kate.

By the time the first jeep lines up, Kate and I are making a reasonable pretence of being fresh, calm and collected. In fact we feel like death warmed up.

'Morning, Mrs Perlmutter. What time would you like breakfast? I see thank you. Have a nice time.'

Rick and Jim are going about the camp busily, getting ready for the departure. If they see us, they show no sign of it. Still, after last night's carrying on, who could blame them. I don't feel guilty about last night, just sad that I should lose Rick like this.

Kate reads my thoughts.

'You weren't ready for Albuquerque yet anyway. Come on, let's go and eat. You've got to feed a hangover.'

CHAPTER 14

Kate and I come to love Mula Mula. The sunrises, the animals, the deep peace of the veldt and forest, as well as the more obvious attractions of people like Mbuna and Ted. But nonetheless, as the time come to move back to Europe, we find ourselves looking forward to it. Although we've had a lot of small trips to organize, to game reserves, and flights in the 747 to South Africa for a weekend, we're a little bored, so the idea of skiing and the High Alps is exciting. I have been skiing once before, and you certainly do meet a nice class of ski instructor up on the mountains.

Pincher tells us that the Firefly château, high in the Maritime Alps, is more of a village really, with an old castle, built by a French eccentric during the last century, converted into a fantastic ski lodge. Everyone will have a personal ski instructor and guide, as well as his own chalet or suite of rooms in the château itself. The day comes when we have to say goodbye to all those who are staying behind, and we load into the Lear jets for the last time. Ted is left on the runway, smiling heroically, but I suspect he is pleased to be able to get on with the animals and the real work after all the frivolity.

Richard is to leave us at Nairobi, and catch a scheduled flight back to London. I am sad to see him go. Despite all the tricks he's played on Kate and me, he's irresistible, a natural winner. And he has no malice in him — it's just that he is totally selfish. Chantal is really much more moved than I am to see the last of him but I don't believe for a moment that it will be the last of him. He's not the sort of person you see the last of. I have grave doubts about what his photo reporting on his visit is going to be about, particularly as he has practically given Lindy the third degree to get all the details out of her about Rip. Still, that's not my responsibility. I just hope for Richard's sake he does nothing to offend Firefly.

Pincher is glad to be back on board the Jumbo. He is now completely in charge again, and he revels in it. His affair with Bridget is cooling off — Kate thinks she may have worn him out. We are to fly to Marseilles before getting into smaller planes with skis attached for our landing in the valley of Haute Brigonne, where the château is. It's completely cut off from the outside world in the winter, and the only way in is by plane or helicopter, although the tycoons aboard are pleased to hear that all the daily stock market prices come in by telex.

On board again, we feel as though we're earning our money once more. Still, we're much more like one big family now, just as Hiram envisaged it, and it's quite hard to get the girls into thinking like stewardesses. After all if you've been drinking, partying and, I'm afraid, sleeping with people for a few weeks it does sort of affect your relationship. It's surprising how few enemies we've made in the process – only one woman whose husband fancies Rosie, has actually made a complaint to Pincher about any of our girls. She's the sort of woman you meet on all flights, tours or holidays, who is convinced she is being put on. It's sad really, because Rosie is a sweet girl who has had great trouble keeping out of her husband's clutches. And we've actually made some dear friends among the women passengers – in my case particularly with Amanda, whose totally despicable character appeals to me. Even Amanda is sad to be moving on, though she has often said that the one great joy of being rich is that you don't have to sleep in the same bed two nights running.

As we hit our cruising speed, Norman gets out his ukelele. He has taught most of these captains of industry his Lancashire songs – in fact he has become the party's cheerleader – and they all sing along as if to the manner born. Perlmutter has promised him a guest appearance on one of his television stations in America. The thought of the good people of Rattlesnake County, Arizona watching Norman Birtwhistle, pigeon fancier, doing an imitation of George Formby, deceased, makes the mind boggle. Still, they've got London Bridge in the next door county, so Perlmutter explains, so why not our Norm?

Everyone is treating me a little bit oddly, for some reason. I get a bit worried.

'Is there anything wrong with me, Kate?'

'Not more than the usual problems, why?'

'Well, everybody's being a bit secretive.'

'Did you use your Lifebuoy this morning?'

'Oh shut up. What you need is a good kick in the pants.'

'Good god, I couldn't. Not after the way Mbuna said goodbye.'

'Kate, not Mbuna?'

'You know me, I like to take in some of the local colour when I go to a place.'

'What's he like?'

'Tish, tish. Put it this way, Kenya are soon going to do as well in the pole vault as in the running.' And off she goes, bottle of champagne in hand.

After dinner, I realize why they've been treating me so oddly. A huge cake comes out of the galley, with twenty-three candles on it. Kate has remembered of course. Norman leads the chorus, and they all shout 'speech'.

I mutter something about what a lot of fun it's been and now that I am old, would they stop making me work so hard.

'We have had a whip round and bought you a little something,' says Jens. Bridget hands me a huge parcel. They are all watching me so eagerly, I am quite sure it's a joke. And I'm quite right. After endless unwrapping, I come to a tiny box of powder. The label reads.

'Powdered rhino horn. Guaranteed effective aphrodisiac. In extreme cases, may be taken undiluted, or applied to the affected part. Product of Kenya.'

The actual presents are embarrassingly generous. I realize that all the girls have really dipped into their pockets, and despite the labels, like the one from Lindy, which reads, 'To our Führer', we really have got a team here. Perlmutter and his wife give me a tenth part of one of their young race-horses, 'and no prizes for guessing which part that is'. Norman explains that if this horse wins the Kentucky Derby, the amount of money my part will make for me at stud is in the millions. 'Trouble is, it's a gelding.' I become a racing fanatic overnight.

'This is the only plane on earth that flies entirely on vintage champagne,' says Pincher.

They allow us to do no work at all. Marseilles at ten in the morning. And yet another hangover. On the runway near our plane are five tiny planes, with retractable skis. We breakfast on board before transferring to these little monsters. They are all painted bright red. The pilots are Swiss and French, and there's a touch of the bloody red baron about them. Our luggage has already gone on ahead by helicopter. It's a beautiful day, bright and clear, with a hint of winter in the air compared with where we've come from. I find it rather exhilarating after the tropics.

As we fly over the foothills of the Alps, the enormous, snow-covered mountains behind frighten me. In this little plane piloted by a swashbuckler called Daniel, with its wretched little skis now extended, we are going to land somewhere in that wasteland. We circle the valley once, and then seem to be flying straight into the side of a mountain. Just as I am convinced that Daniel must be drunk, he flips the stick back and we land on a tiny patch of sloping snow. The force of our landing carries us up a slope and on to another patch of reasonably flat snow. We unload fast, Daniel waves, and launches himself back down the hill. He drops from sight as he comes to the edge and I am fully expecting a crash and some smoke to rise, but in a moment he has gained height again and is speeding away, like an enraged mosquito. The other four planes all do the same, and then here we are, standing like idiots in the middle of the Alps, with nothing but a windsock to show us that the place has ever been seen before by human eyes. Even Pincher is looking a little worried.

'Anyone know 'ow to build an igloo?' asks Norman, who looks daft standing there in his Burton's suit clutching a ukelele. But we are saved from cannibalism and things worse by the appearance of a Sno Kat, a sort of tracked bus.

'Where the hell have you been?' asks Pincher.

'A very small avalanche nearly swept me away,' says the driver of the Sno Kat. 'The others will be here in a moment. 'Appily, I 'ave brought with me some cognac.'

The Frenchman introduces himself all round as, 'Jean-Francois, 'ead instructeur,' and passes around the brandy. It's not cold, except for the feet in the snow, but everyone takes a swig.

We hear the noise of the other Sno Kats approaching.

' 'Ere they are now. Marvellous skiing weather. The best snow of the 'ole season. Jump in now. Allez, allez,' he shouts at the first Sno Kat. Amazing vehicles, like moon-buggies with their tracks. They seem to be able to go over any kind of terrain. This is fortunate, because the slope down to the château is so steep a fly might not be able to cling on for long. As we go down, two of the instructors who came up earlier flash by on skis; they wave and blow us kisses. One flies off the edge of a precipice, his legs and arms extended like a star. The other does a somersault on his skis, and then skis away on one ski.

'The boys are 'appy to see you,' explains Jean-Francois.

'And we are very 'appy to see them,' adds Kate.

With his usual thoroughness, Pincher has had our ski clothes sent on to our rooms. Kate and I are in one vast room in the château, in a turret with a view over miles of mountains. Outside the window, huge icicles are dripping like frozen lollies, and below us the little village, really just an extended farm, surrounds the château. Two tiny streets are feet deep in snow. It's like fairyland – at any moment I expect to see Pincher coming down the road towed by a reindeer.

Pincher is in good form. We all meet in the baronial hall, Kate and I in our own special ski uniforms, all in red, while the other girls are in yellow. Pincher explains what is available for the benefit of the guests.

'This is the largest privately controlled ski area in the world. During the winter no one can get up here except by plane or helicopter. There are no roads. You can ski every day of course, or you can walk, hunt chamois sheep, climb, or skate. Over in the old barn we have a heated swimming pool and a sauna. Now a word about the skiing. We at Firefly have presented you with a real challenge. For the beginners there is a long, gentle slope with an easy lift. For the more expert, your guide will take you each day in a Sno Kat or by helicopter to ski some of the most exciting ski trails in the world. Please let Jean-Francois know how, and when you wish to ski. Most of you have sent your own skis on, but for those who are new to the game, we will be fitting you with the finest equipment money can buy. Now ladies and gentlemen, the Château Brigonne welcomes you to the High Alps.'

Lunch is out of this world. It makes the last time I went skiing seem like a visit to a health farm; goose, venison, endless pâtés and terrines, fresh vegetables and fish, flown in daily from Marseilles. Kate and I spend the afternoon in familiarization, while the guests set off to try out the slopes.

By all accounts they are fantastic. Jens, who is of course a superb skiier, goes off in a helicopter with two guides, and comes back much later in a state of high excitement. On the gentle slopes right outside the château, expensive bottoms in beautiful ski clothes are denting the snow. But waiters appear with jugs of heated wine, and there is always a handsome instructor near by with a helping hand. And on the terrace, Helga and Chantal sit with their faces turned up to the sun as though they were praying to it. Later they go to the ice rink, where they skate, hand in hand for hours.

We soon fall into the way of life. As Kate explains it, it is ridiculous to be paid for doing something you can't afford to do yourself. We are even allowed to ski every morning for a few hours, along with the guests. Now I don't want to be indelicate, but there is something about skiing that makes you randy. It's all that exercise and all those devilishly handsome, sun-bronzed ski instructors, with muscles like whipcord under their tight ski pants. Kate and I go skiing with Norman and Madge every morning. The other girls are mostly quite good, apparently having learned to ski in New Mexico, which sounds like a tall tale to me, but they are all better than us, and skiing is something you don't learn in books, so perhaps you can ski in New Mexico. Norman thinks the object of skiing is to get from the top to the bottom in the shortest time taking the straightest line. This is a good theory, except that if you don't know how to stop, which Norman doesn't, it's very dangerous.

But I digress. I was saying that skiing makes you randy. Our instructor, Thierry, or Terry as we call him, is a very silent, endlessly patient young boy, normally a farmer, but something of a star on skis on account of the fact that he lived in these mountains all his twenty-one years. Kate and I, infected by the general air of lech about the place, institute a 'get Thierry' competition, winner to be served breakfast in bed by the loser, with of course, Thierry there as evidence of success. Poor Thierry. Good looking though he is, and accomplished skiier though he is, he cannot understand why we keep falling over when he is near. As he helps me out of the snow for the fourth time this morning, I rub my breasts against his arm and give him a little kiss of thanks.

'What are you up to,' asks Norm, 'trying to divert him from the paths of righteousness? All Mother's Boys, these froggies.

116

Come here, lad, help get this sapling from out of me jumper.'

Old Norman is so tangled up with a future giant of the forest that Jean-Francois has to lift him bodily out of the snow, unbend the tree, shake the snow out of Norman's trousers, dust off his Fair Isle sweater, and clean his goggles before Norm even knows which way he is pointing. No, Penny, I think to myself, you've got to be more cunning than this. Funny thing is, with all the men in the place baying around like starving wolves, Jean-Francois doesn't seem to fancy us. I can't understand it.

That night we are all going on a torchlit sleigh ride to a cabin about a mile up the track, right in the heart of the forest, for a fondue bourguignonne and lots of hot wine. Tonight has to be the night. I plan my strategy carefully. All the other girls, bar Kate and I, seem to have met with success. In fact Bridget, in her usual fashion, is on close terms with half the village already. But what is wrong with Thierry. If I knew that, I could win our bet. I am sure. I am tempted to ask Amanda, who is running Bridget a close second in that particular race, but last time I asked her for help she took the whole problem to her bosom so to speak. No there is a clue to this somewhere.

After we have all drunk our last glass of framboise, a sort of sweet but heady liqueur, we go out to the sleigh. They are covered in great big furry rugs. By a bit of blatant barging, I manage to sit next to Thierry under the rug. Some of the instructors ski down the mountain ahead of us, carrying torches. It amazes me that most of them can ski at all, let alone in the dark and carrying a torch, after the way they've been knocking it back. I let my thigh touch Thierry's under the rug. He seems preoccupied, so I let my hand rest as if by accident on his leg.

'My goodness it's cold, il est froid, oui?'

'Oui.'

'Here, feel my hands.' He tries to get his hand out, but I hang on to it. With far less excuse than this, I've known men who would have stripped off and been burrowing under that rug as though they were prospecting for oil by now. But not Thierry. My hand steals over the front of his trousers.

'You don't like me.'

'Penny, I like you very much.'

117

'What's the matter, then?'

'You promise you will not tell the other instructeurs?'

'Promise.'

'I am, how you call it, impotent.'

The way he says it, I think he is saying 'important'.

'Of course you are. We're all important in our own way. I bet your father is the mayor or something. But because you are important, surely . . .'

'Non, non, impotent.'

'Ah, yes well, that's altogether more serious.'

'In France, it is a great disgrace, to be impotent.'

'Well, it's not exactly an honour in England.'

'Can I talk to you?'

'Sure. Come up to my room.'

Thierry tells me the whole tale; I don't think he's incurable by any means. It seems that he had a nasty experience with one of his sister's friends as a lad and he has never been able to get it together since. In fact for the last two years, he has stayed away from girls altogether. When the story got out, he had to leave his village.

I get him into bed, and really I don't know where to begin. He is so grateful that I haven't mocked him or tried therapy on him – apparently most girls just think you have to be persistent and something will happen. So we sleep like brother and sister. I put the 'Do not disturb' sign on the door.

In the morning Kate appears with a marvellous breakfast, orange juice, croissants, tartines and various jams. She shakes my hand.

'Let me be the first to congratulate you.'

I accept her compliments with a good grace. Thierry peeps nervously out from under the bedclothes. Poor lad, he thinks all English people shake hands at breakfast time with their close friends. Actually, he is absolutely gorgeous, but what can I do to help him? I don't know. I decide to ask Amanda after all.

'Perhaps he needs an older woman.'

'I thought you might say that.'

'Well, it's a question of confidence. I mean one of my son's friends was just the same.'

'Your son's friends?'

'Everybody is somebody's son,' she says, 'or daughter. Darling, I have had so many husbands that I am related to half the blue bloods in America. If I had to keep my hands off all of them, I might as well take the veil. So I make it a rule not to try and figure out blood lines when I am going to hop in to the sack with somebody.'

'Well, OK, see what you can do.'

I don't know what Amanda does do, but the next day Thierry is transformed. He gives me a kiss on the slopes, touches up Kate as he helps her on to the lift, and even gets poor Madge in a flutter.

'What the hell have you done to him?'

'Just the way they're all affected by me.'

'What you have done is turn him into yet another nasty little Romeo. I liked him the way he was.'

Kate's right. We liked him because he was shy and retiring. Now he's insufferable. Still, that night I find out what Amanda has taught him. A lot for one night, it seems. When we are undressed he immediately leaps on me like a starving man on a crust of bread. What he lacks in finesse, he certainly makes up in vigour. Soon the bedsprings are singing like a choir of crickets. He's trying to make up for lost time, because by first light he still shows no signs of wanting to sleep for more than about ten minutes at a time.

I am a pale shadow on the ski slopes. I tell you what, I say, I think you should talk more to my friend Bridget, you would like her. She majored in French at Albuquerque Junior High School.

'Bridget, I think you should ski with Thierry. You have a lot in common. He studied English in his junior high school.'

'Well that's terrific. Vous parlez anglais tres bien.'

Thierry smirks like the cat that's about to get the cream, and I leave them Parlez-vousing their little heads off.

CHAPTER 15

For me, our weeks at Château Brigonne are bliss. The weather is wonderful, hardly a cloud in the sky by day and fresh snow at night. Which, I come to learn, is the only way to ski. Even with just a couple of hours every morning, Kate and I become quite good. Kate falls forward and I fall backwards, but otherwise we're about equal. Kate explains that her particular structure falling forward is almost a law of physics.

'So I suppose I fall backwards because I've got a big bottom?' I ask.

'Well I wouldn't say it was big, I mean I saw a bigger one only last year, well perhaps the year before. No it's certainly not the biggest I've ever seen.'

Really, if I say it myself, all this exercise, both on and off the slopes has put Kate and me in terrific shape. And when you are feeling and looking good, it seems to heighten your sexual awareness. At least that's my excuse. Although I'll never be in Bridget's league, I'm not doing badly. Bridget and Thierry look like a pair of boxers at the end of fifteen rounds, both wishing they could throw in the sponge, but hoping the bell will rescue them. A great bit of casting that, on my part. When Greek meets Greek, if I remember my Keats or somebody, which I don't.

I come to know Jens very, very well. Neither of his girls is much interested in skiing, so I often go with him. He's a little too old to ski at the lunatic speeds the instructors do, but he skis beautifully, and waits ages for me sometimes to negotiate the tricky bits. Our favourite run is to the top of a nearby mountain by helicopter, then we follow a long gentle path down. There's lots of opportunity for Jens to ski steeper bits while I just swish sedately down.

Near the end of our stay in Brigonne, we ski this run, stopping at a little shepherd's hut with a balcony for a drink and some crusty bread. Something of his youth has come out in Jens again, skiing, and he's the proper little boy scout with his bag and thermos flask and sandwiches.

The sun is gloriously hot, and I strip off to my bra and we make a cradle of skis to lie against. Since that night in Mula Mula I haven't been to bed with Jens. The way he carries on, I am not even sure he remembers who was in on his scene that night. As we lie in the sun, he begins to tell me about his life.

'The most important thing is never to miss opportunities. I am terrified that if I shut my eyes for one second, something will happen that I miss. You are young, never miss an opportunity, and I am not talking just about sex. Do you understand me, yes?'

That conversation, high up in the mountains with this famous man, makes a deep impression on me. I realize for the first time, I suppose, that he is not just a pleasure-loving, rich, successful film star (as if that weren't enough?) but really a man who is searching, striving.

'Jens, tell me, I mean you know everybody, and have been everywhere, what's left for you?'

'Making love to you in the snow.'

He begins to caress my breasts, and then unfastens my ski pants. This is like my boyhood in the Tyrol, except that lederhosen were even more difficult to get off than these stretchpants.

We must look an absolutely ludicrous sight to any watching chamois sheep. Two naked figures, or nearly naked, except for ski boots, with their trousers round their ankles. The cold snow is beginning to bite into my bottom as he caresses me. I don't even want to think how many times he has done this, I am just grateful that I can enjoy it without inhibition or fear. As he enters me, I seize him tight. He makes love slowly deeply, until I cry out with joy. Jens is talking to himself in German. He lies back in the snow and I roll over next to him and kiss him, so tenderly. There is a tear in his eye, or perhaps it's just from the cold snow, but he lies staring at the mountains until I fear for him.

'Come on, Jens, what would your fan club say if you got it frostbitten.

It makes him laugh and the moment passes. Jens never pretends about anything, and this is no more than a pleasant interlude for him, but for a moment I am sure I have seen the real Jens, a man the world doesn't even suspect exists.

The rest of the week passes all too quickly, and it's time to head off again to Greece. Jens is a little distant, as if he wants me to forget his moment of doubt, or weakness. For the last few weeks, all the good skiers have been taking flights in the little planes to other resorts and snowfields, some in Switzerland, some in Italy, so we have got used to the planes with their wild pilots. Even so, dropping off the edge of the cliff is a terrifying sensation. There's a good second before they pick up power and gain altitude again.

Daniel pats my knee reassuringly.

'Sometime I fall all the way down there, to that forest, before the engine she go. I nearly sheet myself.'

Greece is golden, hot and, if possible, even more fantastic than the other two Firefly resorts. Hiram has bought an island with an old monastery and village. It looks like paradise. Whitewashed cottages, the simple exteriors giving no clue to the beautiful cool, whitewashed interiors. It's called 'Ekinos', which Pincher, ever a mine of information, says is Greek for starfish. It would be boring of me to go over all the little touches that The Firefly Organization has thought up for this last leg of the trip. Suffice it to say that they have excelled themselves. We have much more to do here, because there are so many possibilities, – flights and boat trips to the islands, waterskiing, shopping expeditions, sailing and lots of other activities to organize. For the first week Kate and I hardly get a chance to get our bikinis on, let alone wet.

After the first week, things slow down a bit and I go with some of the party on an old Greek fishing boat that has been converted as a cruiser. We are to go for a few days round some of the nearby Islands, Skiathos, Mikonos and others. This boat or caique as Jens tells me it should be called, is hundreds of years old. It has been converted to sleep six, and the crew, all two of them, sleep on the deck under a tarpaulin if its raining, and under the stars if it's not. It's a lazy, dreamy way of getting about, because without the motor its one sail only makes about three knots. I am deputed to be cook, and the Perlmutters, Norman, Madge, Jens and his two girls come along.

Pincher is beside himself with anxiety, because the boat was never meant for cruises, just overnight stays at places where there is a proper hotel and restaurant, mostly at other islands. He is dead worried that I am going to poison some of his guests.

'None of this is scheduled, you know.'

We set off at a pace that an ox would find relaxing, and head due north towards Skiathos. The captain is called Aramis, and his mate, who is twelve, is called Joe by everyone. Normally, when not on the high seas, Joe is a donkey-minder by profession. Aramis is a local favourite with the girls, taller than most Greeks, with a sort of goldeny brown hair. He loves the old boat.

'How long to Skiathos, Aramis?'

He shrugs. 'One day, maybe two days.'

I prepare a simple lunch of cheese, huge tomatoes, greek bread and olives. After the splendours of the cooking for the past few months, I am surprised that everyone seems to lap it up. Old Norman is something of an expert on Greek food, having been twice to the Nicosia Taverna in Blackburn. Aramis produces a gallon of retsina from the cool hold of the ship. We spend the rest of the day dozing, lying in the sun and drinking retsina.

As night falls, we anchor close to an island in a little cove. Aramis is all for going ashore, because he knows a wonderful taverna in the village. It seems unlikely, because there are only about five houses visible, and pulled up on the beach are two or three fishing boats.

'My cousin. You come with me.'

We paddle ashore. In the tiny square of the village are a church, a couple of houses, and the taverna. It is a simple place. Aramis is greeted like a returning hero, tables are laid in the street under a vine, and we begin to eat and nibble olives and other little snacks. Raki is the local choice of tipple, and who are we to argue? We cause a sensation. I realize that I am virtually naked, wearing only a pair of Levi shorts and a tiny halter top, by the standards of the village. But Helga and Chantal make me look overdressed. They are both wearing see-through Greek peasant blouses, and their breasts are quite visible. They don't mind, Jens doesn't mind, and the local populace love it. Aramis is like a general running a campaign. He introduces Jens, who even in this remote part of the world is known, to the mayor, who is also a relation. He puts his arm on my shoulder as if to suggest to the locals that we will be man and wife soon, and he sends little Joe racing back and forth to the kitchen for more raki, more quails, more wine. Little Joe doesn't stop running for a moment. By the time dinner has arrived, the whole village, numbering about fifty, is gathered round us. Norman sends Joe to get his ukelele. The bazouki players come into the open and we dance and sing and eat the night away. The food is quite delicious, mountains of taramasalata, fresh prawns, and grilled lamb.

We girls are much in demand with the younger men of the village, who have got a little fed up with the Greek custom of men dancing with each other. We leap and waltz all over the place. Madge and the mayor do a foxtrot of sorts. She's trotting at least, as he swoops around the patio. Plates begin to fly, Jens sings a song and Mrs Perlmutter has to be rescued from a nearby cottage from the arms of a randy fisherman.

Perlmutter thinks this is a great joke.

'For Chrissake don't rescue her, she would pay good money for that. Better get the boy to a clinic, his eyesight must be failing.'

Actually, Mrs Perlmutter is not quite sure whether she wants to be rescued or not, but there are no hard feelings. In a moment the same boy has Madge in an embrace that the Boston Strangler would be proud of and is edging her towards his cottage, like a hermit crab, appearing to go one way but actually scuttling in quite a different direction.

This party is heading for some sort of climax. I am nestling happily against the brown, lean body of our skipper, when three jeeps and some vans race into the square their lights blazing, and white-helmeted soldiers or police leap out, waving machine guns menacingly. Aramis steps forward to explain, but they chuck him into a van, all the men in another, the locals, or some of them in another.

'I suppose we'll be raped and tortured,' says Helga happily.

'I won't be raped or tortured. I'll tell them I'm a friend of Gracie Fields' niece,' says Madge. She's getting a little confused by the quick change of scene.

'Do you know, my husband owns three Greek companies,' adds Mrs Perlmutter. 'As soon as they see who we are, they'll let us out.'

When they do get a close look at us in the barracks, it only confirms their worst suspicions. Three near-naked girls, two of them actually arm-in-arm, two middle-aged ladies, both plastered, one little fellow with his trousers rolled up to his knees and a suspicious object under his arm, Jens, gloriously drunk doing his imitation of himself in his greatest role, and finally Perlmutter who is laughing so much he has to sit down, which earns him a kick in the arse. Of our Greek friends, we see nothing.

One man, obviously the most senior policeman, comes forward. He tries to make us understand something, but it's hopeless. As the representative of the Firefly Organization, I say 'Ekinos' a few times, but the look on the policeman's face suggests that anyone who could talk about starfish at a time like this is obviously insane. We girls are led to a cell, where we wait for something to happen. Two policemen come in and tell us, by sign language to strip. As between us we don't have enough clothes to make a respectable handkerchief, it seems a little unnecessary.

'They seem to like you best,' says Helga. 'Perhaps because you are bigger than us.'

It is true that the two policemen are staring rather intently at my breasts as though expecting them to reveal a secret of some sort. Apart from my nipples getting rather hard in embarrassment, little happens. Helga and Chantal think the whole thing is hilarious. Despite the fact that they start pouting and posing, the two policemen soon leave, saying 'Hello' for some reason.

From the next cell we hear the ukelele start up. If that doesn't get us released, nothing will. Nothing does. We are still there in the morning. We gather that they are trying to telephone Athens. By lunch time, Athens still hasn't been found. I am not worried in any physical sense, it's just that I feel a responsibility for the guests. Still, lunch isn't bad for a prison, lots of bread and salami and even a glass of wine.

'I like it here,' says Chantal. Every hour or so, we are made to strip and somebody new is brought to look at us. I suspect they are selling tickets at the door. Even Helga and Chantal get a little tired of taking off their blouses and pants. I begin to understand what it feels like to work in Soho.

Just when I start to wonder if we will ever be released, or

spend the rest of our lives doing a quick change routine, we hear a mighty roaring overhead. It sounds like a helicopter. It is. There is a lot of shouting, and I hear Pincher's voice, invoking the name of the American ambassador, NATO, Christendom, world peace, and Firefly.

We are all released. A man with so much scrambled egg on his uniform he looks like a Panamian general, is shouting at the poor policemen, who are formed up like naughty boys. He turns to us, and makes a little speech.

'My dear friends, I apologize on the behalf of the Greek people for this terrible confusion. These policemen have been looking out for smugglers, and last night they thought that you were some of those. They are very ignorant people out here in the islands. If they had known you were our distinguished visitors, this would never have happened. But nobody visits this poor island. I do apologize.'

Jens makes a moving speech on our behalf, apologizing in his turn if we have caused offence by our behaviour, but, as he puts it:

'The warmth and the friendliness of your charming people overcame our normal restraint.'

Stirring stuff. I expect everyone to clap, and for a moment Jens does as well. Pincher then makes a short speech, Chantal and Helga kiss everyone in sight, and we are returned to Pincher's care. He wants us all to come back by helicopter. Only Mrs Permutter accepts; her narrow escape from rapine has made her heart flutter. The rest of us feel as though we've been through a war and come out ahead. We march back to our boat like the prisoners on the River Kwai, singing our own national anthem, composed by Jens with musical accompaniment by Norman. Poor Aramis has had a rather hard time in his cell, but he is still smiling, despite one black eye. It turns out little Joe was the hero. He immediately ran away when the police came, borrowed a fishing boat and set sail for Ekinos. Pincher, after restraining a perfectly understandable impulse to bomb the island, summoned a senior Greek Army Officer and they set off to extricate us.

As we sail away from the island, the villagers line up and wave. Jens stands in the bows, occasionally taking a swig from a raki bottle, and waving back.

'That island was on the verge of a community gang bang

that would have made history in these parts. It would have entered Greek folklore – then those goddamned police arrived,' he says sadly.

We nurse Aramis's black eye and other wounds. There's nothing much wrong with him, but he likes attention. Little Joe is a perfectly adequate skipper anyway and he's the only one who stays sober for the rest of our voyage.

CHAPTER 16

The good ship *Raki,* as we come to call her for fairly obvious reasons, sails away towards Skiathos, while Pincher flies back to Ekinos. He has asked us to keep in touch on the radio, every day, without fail, or you're fired, Penny. I point out that I haven't the slightest clue how to work the radio, which seems to be used exclusively to hang Aramis's naval type cap on until we approach a port. I am not at all sure that Aramis knows how to use the radio, either, but he assures me he does. Anyway, between bouts of resting, he struggles with it every morning and evening until he has worked up a good sweat. He seems to be speaking to the Turkish Admiralty a lot, which is not the idea at all. Sometimes he gets in touch with a shrimp fishing fleet, and once with an American submarine, but never, to my knowledge, with Pincher.

'You know what will happen, don't you?' asks Perlmutter, 'some goddam Russki will think we are a spy boat and come and blow us out of the water. Little maritime accident. We'll rate one line in the Lloyd's shipping register. Tell the idiot to leave the goddam radio alone.'

Skiathos is very pleasant. We buy all the things you are supposed to buy, but there are too many people around who recognize Jens so after a boozy lunch we set sail again, roughly in the direction of Ekinos, with a few stop-overs. Little Joe points at an angle about ninety-five degrees south of where Aramis is heading, and after a low, fierce, discussion, Aramis alters course. Thank God for Joe, I say, but I don't confide my fears to the others. I mean a skipper who doesn't know the way is about as useless as the Pope's prick, as the saying goes. Still he's a lovely fellow, Aramis, and he likes a drink. Joe is under the drinking age, fortunately, or we would still be out cruising in the Aegean now, I shouldn't wonder.

That night we meet another yacht. She is very long, low and elegant. But something is amiss. I realize what it is. They are sailing under the power of one tiny sail in the front, which seems a pity, as the wind is carrying the cumbersome Raki along beautifully.

Someone on deck waves to us, and we come alongside. Aramis takes half the paint off their boat, but the gentleman who has called to us doesn't seem to mind.

'You need any help?' asks Jens.

'Shit no, not unless you got some good grass on board,' says the other figure who is bearded, with hair halfway down his back. For one moment I think he may be in a round the world race, or something.

'You sailing this thing all on your own,' asks Perlmutter.

'Hell no, the others are all stoned downstairs in the caboose. Come aboard.'

We both cast anchor. The yacht is called *American Freak* I notice, as we clamber over the side. The rest of the crew are two more men and two girls, all of them lying in a huge cabin, which looks as though it must have been very plush before the hurricane struck. There are half-empty cans, bottles of every known drink, cigarette papers, books, comics, tennis shoes, and a mini motorcycle, in bits, lying around everywhere. And above it all rises the pungent odour of grass.

'Hi, I'm Hamilton Grover the third,' says the one lying on the floor. 'This is my yacht, and what I say is law. Trouble is nobody gives a shit about the law around here. Come on in and have a joint.'

Hamilton Grover the third is a very weird young man, the son, presumably, of Hamilton Grover the second, Perlmutter knows him in business. He owns half of Pittsburgh, or somewhere like that.

'If you hang on a while, we were just about to eat something, why don't you join us?'

We do. After a while the whole party gets very matey, what with the pot and the booze and the excellent curry one of the girls makes. Norman declines a smoke, but tucks into the curry, nearly as good as the Moti Mahal in Blackburn, he rates it.

The yacht, underneath the mess, is quite fantastic. It has stereo in every cabin, a bar, a large galley, even a shower and a sauna.

'My old man gave me this as a twenty-first present and told me to get the hell out. That was two years ago. This is really spaced out, man. How about some hash brownies, Julie?'

'Where have you been in the last two years?' I ask, though I am beginning to feel a little funny.

'Well when we wake up in the morning we just head off somewhere, anywhere. Sometimes we don't go anywhere at all. It depends.'

Peter Kolsen, the one who greeted us, tells us that what they are really doing at the moment is diving for a wreck. They think they have found an ancient argosy, which I always thought was a magazine, but which Louis, the third boy, explains is a ship. By now the conversation is getting a little confused anyway, as the stereo is so loud it is impossible to hear what the person next to you is saying. Chantal and Helga start to dance together, in their own special way, syncopated like two of the Supremes. Lewis and I go for a stroll on the deck.

'I haven't seen a television or a movie for years, but I am sure I recognize that guy, the older one with the two chicks.'

I explain who he is. And I try to explain what we are all doing, but it's not easy. Suddenly Norman comes up on deck. He strips off, and leaps over the side.

'Those hash brownies of Julie's are fantastic. Always grabs them like this.'

Norman can't actually swim, without a foot on the ground, so I dive in after him, Louis dives in after me, and, stoned as we are, we keep Norman afloat until the others can throw a rope to us.

'I just suddenly knew I could swim,' says Norman happily.

'Well you were wrong.'

'I feel spaced right out, lass.'

'Have another cookie.'

'No he won't, there's drugs in them things.' Madge has come to supervise the drying out of Norman. She's cackling like an old leghorn that's about to lay a peacock's egg. Together they get off to the Raki, Norman saying he's going to drop out from society and open a fish and chip shop in Skiathos.

In the cabin again, I strip off and somebody lends me a T-shirt, which is all I wear. It's quite a long one fortunately. It seems to turn Aramis on, however, and he tries to get me to go back to the Raki.

'You go and I'll see you in a moment.' Aramis staggers off, shouts at little Joe, who helps him to bed, which is on the deck.

'This wreck we found is full of gold coins; trouble is with these Greeks, if you find anything like that they take the lot and give you a small percentage, so we're going to get the hell out of Greek waters when we've loaded up. Come with me.'

Pete shows me down a stairway. In a store room they have a pile of coins, about the size of a small saucer. The ones that have been cleaned are shining gold.

'Those must be worth a fortune.'

'They are. Hell, we don't need the money, but they sure are beautiful. Look at this.'

He gives me one, a small gold piece with a hole in the middle.

'You can wear it as a necklace, look, like mine.'

He is wearing his coin on a leather thong.

'Here let me fix it.'

There's not a lot of room in the store and he seems to be having trouble getting the thong round my neck. My nipples are standing up hard through the T-shirt.

'Oh shit, let's do the necklace another time.' His hands go to my breasts, and he begins to rub them softly. He's a nice little fellow, this Peter, what I can see of him under the hair. Soon he has his hands under the T-shirt, and he starts caressing me gently.

I am almost dreaming: the grass has made me feel as though I am watching all this going on, not actually taking part. I see him undo his shorts, and see my hands go to him down there. I am not one for thinking the male member is a thing of special beauty, but this one certain is trying. He puts his hands under my bottom and lifts me on to the table with the coins, and then, standing up, he slips into me. I feel as though I am going to burst, and him such a little fellow, too. My head and body seem to have parted company, although my hips are grinding away urgently. Suddenly I start to laugh.

'What's so funny?' asks Pete, then he starts laughing too.

131

It's all so stupid, me sitting on a table, getting splinters in my bum, with this man I hardly know, and I am so stoned I feel I am about to float away.

The two of us laugh like maniacs.

'Come, let's go to my cabin,' he says, and he hops down the corridor his shorts round his ankles, giggling like a child. His cabin is a terrible mess, but we burrow down amongst the clothes and jumbled up blankets, sleeping bags and a snorkel appears.

'What do you use that for?' I ask, as he begins, to caress me again.

'What do you think?' Quick as a flash.

'I just wouldn't know.'

'I'm a rubber fetishist. I hate diving but I do love the wet suit.'

I kiss him all over, and he tastes very salty. He is truly enormous – so big that I can hardly get it in my mouth.

'That's beautiful, oh yes, terrific.'

I begin to laugh again, and nearly choke myself. I pull him on top of me.

'Right, you can do the work now.'

He makes love slowly and deliberately, never stopping, until the rhythm and intensity reach bursting point. We both come at once, but I spoil the moment by beginning to laugh again.

'That's the funniest lay I ever had,' says Pete, and we both burst out again. I don't know what it is they put in their curry, but it really blows my mind. The rest of the night is frightening. I begin to laugh hysterically, uncontrollably, until I am so weak I can barely breathe.

At one moment Jens is there. He holds my hand and his presence is a great help.

'Don't worry, baby, you're having a trip, you'll be OK, I'm here.' At last I sleep, but without Jens there I don't know what I would do. It seems as though there is a great void into which I could fall, and never stop falling. I am very frightened.

By the lunchtime the next day, I am more or less down, as these people say. Just a little acid, baby, nothing to worry about. But for me it was terrifying. It really only got to Norman and me, for some reason, and Norman is feeling terrible this morning. But we feel quite proud of ourselves in a way. But I swear I will never knowingly take LSD after that.

Pete is very apologetic.

'It's that Julie, she put some acid in the coffee you had. Thought you would like it, silly bitch. Your little friend Norman as well.'

Pete calls up Ekinos on their radio, and I talk to Pincher, dutiful servant that I am.

'Come on home, we've got a surprise for you.'

'What is it?'

'You come and see.'

We leave *American Freak* lying at anchor. Only Pete is up and about. The others are all still in bed even though it's nearly three o'clock?

'How long to Ekinos, Aramis?'

'Three hours, four hours.'

'Two hours,' says Joe, who is right as usual. Aramis looks as though he would like to kick his little arse right out of the Aegean; nobody likes a know-all, but in this case I am very grateful we've got one on board. *American Freak* recedes fast into the distance, only the sounds of the stereo linger on. We make very good speed, running before, as Jens explains it, is what these boats are good at. Almost exactly two hours later, the low, white profile of Ekinos comes into view.

'I told you two hours,' says Aramis.

He makes a great show of docking the boat, ordering Joe around, but Joe is a man with time on his side. He doesn't care. After living comparatively rough for a few days, it's great to be back. Everyone wants to hear our adventures. I lie in a hot bath telling Kate all about it. She's taken up with the waterski instructor, who struts up and down the beach hoping somebody will try and kick sand in his eyes. Nobody does.

'Have you tried it on waterskis yet?'

'What sort of company have you been mixing in, my girl to talk to a young lady like that?'

I tell her about *American Freak*. Kate, of course has heard of Hamilton Grover.

'Why didn't you bring him back with you, and a little one for me, perhaps?'

'I did bring something back.'

'What's that?'

I fish into the water between my breasts and pull out the gold coin. Kate is so eager to see it that she practically ends up in the bath with me.

'Good God, that's Roman,' she says. 'Imperator Justinius. It must be worth a fortune.'

'I hope it is. Still it's also very pretty and will remind me of Peter Kolsen.'

'Yes, gold is the way to a girl's knickers.'

'Do you mind. Look, what's the surprise Pincher told me about earlier?'

'Well, surprise is perhaps a little strong. Shock may be a .better word to describe this person.'

'It's a person is it. Let me guess, not Scottish by any chance, not unconnected with the photographic trade?'

'Got it in one. Richard has arrived to do another article.'

'How did the last one go down?'

'A world-wide scoop, the death of an idol, and his love for a simple girl. Illustrated with pictures of Mula Mula. Great for business, so Pincher says, and you are in it.'

'What has he said. Nothing too saucy, I hope?'

'Not about your sex life, dear, just a few quotes from you about Rip's last moments.'

'Oh that is sad. He's such an exploiter.'

The exploiter chooses this moment to march into the bathroom. He bends down to kiss me, reaches into the water and tweaks a nipple. He's so damned cocky, I can't resist pulling him in head first into the bath. Kate helps with a push, just as he's poised. He emerges from the water, cigar in his mouth, and sits in the bath as though he were at home on a favourite armchair.

'Hello, how have you been?'

'Fine, thank you, Richard, not missing you at all. I hear you are a world-wide success through your exploitation of innocent people.'

'Darling, your boss thinks I am the greatest thing since sliced bread. My pictures have made these tours world famous, and me very rich.'

'What's the next story about?'

'We'll have to see. I mean it's not every day you're able to take pictures of the last resting place of a pop idol. Perhaps this time I'll do something with a bit of human interest. Like the drowning of Penny Sutton, deceased air stewardess.'

As he says it, he ducks me, and pulls in Kate too. He's so quick we find all three of us sitting in one large bath in a flash. He hops out of the bath and comes back with a bottle of champagne, which he solemnly opens, and then he's back in the bath. We drink it in a very dignified manner, though there's a lot of water running out of the end of his cigar. Kate looks stunning in her purple smock. I don't really feel dressed for the occasion at all, though my gold coin is admired by all. Richard takes a picture of me and Kate in the bath, which is one of my favourite souvenirs of Ekinos to this day. It seems to sum up the feeling of the place so well.

With Richard about, dinner is a riot. He and Jens go in for a Greek plate-breaking competition, till all the dining area is covered with bits of smashed crockery. These two break about ten dozen plates between them but Pincher, though I know he's dying inside, shows very little pain through his smile. The evening is marred only by Mrs Perlmutter, whose near miss with Mediterranean sex has unbalanced her, or as Perlmutter puts it 'scrambled her brains'. Perlmutter has to take her to bed after she tries to strip on the table, hitting poor Madge a glancing blow with a shoe discarded carelessly.

'I hope that shoe's all right,' says Norman, 'it must have had quite a shock hitting something as hard as that.'

I can't stop laughing, and Kate has to leave the room, though perhaps the fact that the demon water-skier is champing at the bit outside has something to do with it. I get a moment to thank Jens for helping me through my bad trip, and he says:

'It was nothing. I am glad you did it, so at least you know what it's like. I used to do a lot of it, but I think it does scramble your brains, as old Perlmutter says. There are quite a few household names in Hollywood who are completely spaced out. Dat's terrible. You're going to lose your faculties soon enough without helping yourself on the way.'

Amanda is very gushy:

'I've missed you, honey, I sure do wish I was along, but you know that boy who looks after the scuba diving, well he's been looking after your Aunt Mandy for the last few days and I didn't want to leave him. Nice boy. I've given him a boat so he can set up on his own next season.'

135

'Does that mean you're finished with him.'

'Finish is a strong word, honey, but the truth is, something better came along.'

'Oh yes, and what was that?'

'Well it was the photographer boy, that one there breaking plates.'

'Amanda, that's four of my boy-friends you've had already on this trip.'

'Honey, I didn't know he was a particular friend of yours. I thought you liked that Rick, the pilot. Anyway, way he tells it, you and he are just good friends.'

'He exaggerates.'

'Penny, honey, for a very rich woman, I have very left-wing views about property. As far as men are concerned, I believe the good ones should be common property for all women. Let the bank clerks and the accountants go off to their little homes at night, but men like Richard, they have a duty to perform to women of spirit all over the world, and I'm gonna go on exacting that duty as long as I can. How's my nose looking, by the way? I think I may have it slightly hooked when I get back to the States. More character, everyone's doing it. I mean you would look terrific with slightly baggy eyes. No, this year it's character in faces that's in.'

'Amanda, as a friend, I must warn you that Richard will be looking for a story.'

'Let him look. He tries to publish any pictures of me without my consent, he'll have an army of lawyers trampling over his grave. Listen honey, one of my husbands was in the rackets. I can get that boy removed from view if he gives trouble.'

Funny thing is, I know she means it. In my experience the rich don't get rich by accident. Mostly they have a quality of determination that is denied to lesser mortals like myself. I am determined not to talk to Richard again, but I find myself, much later, not merely talking to him, but in bed with him, even though I know he's come hot-foot (or other parts) from Amanda. My New Year's resolution is going to be more determination. Fortunately New Year is a long way off.

CHAPTER 17

All good things come to an end, as the philosopher said. And Ekinos is almost too good to be true. Kate is particularly fond of Greek men by the end of our stay. As I think I've said earlier, she's always been one for the Latin type. I discover something about them too, namely that once you get over all the masculine ego bit, some of them are very nice, much like anybody else, in fact. We are in a special position, of course, being passers in the night, that the local women will never achieve. Aramis has a wife on another island and when the season is over, he is going to go back and sit waiting for the summer, while she does all the work. And probably telling a few stories about the blonde English girl he met who fell for his charms. Actually, I quite like him, but I'm glad he has to spend most of his time down at the little harbour, because he can be very possessive.

Kate has gone rather quiet the last two weeks, because she says she is in love with her water-ski instructor. I must say, as a piece of prime beef, he is fantastic; Kate finds the sight of him skiing backwards on one ski thrilling, but as I point out to her, it's not really a talent you can package and sell in England. A strange thing has happened to Norman – he has also fallen in love. Madge doesn't seem to mind. The girl in question is one of the chambermaids, not more than sixteen, who loves to hear Norman sing. She is round and fat, with dark curly hair, and Norman becomes her idol. I wonder if she doesn't think he's Cliff Richard disguised as an older man, such is her devotion.

'Penny, you've got to help me.'

'What is it, Norman?'

'I'm in love with Maria.'

'That's nice for you.'

'Look, lass, be serious. I want to marry her.'

'What?'

'I want to marry her, and come and live out here.'

'What about Madge?'

'Madge hasn't really taken to the international life like me. We could never settle here together.'

'What about your horse-racing? And the dogs? And the pigeons?'

'Bugger the bloody pigeons.'

'Well, what am I supposed to do to help?'

'When we set off back to the United States, I am going to stay behind.'

'Yes?'

'Yes, and you are going to make the arrangements and then tell our Madge. I've already told Maria.'

'Ta, Norman, but I can't do it. You'll have to tell her yourself.'

Really! when I think about it, it doesn't seem such a bad idea. Old Perlmutter would certainly give Norman the money to open a small business of some sort, he's also devoted to Norman, and Maria would probably cook or something very well. And to cap it all, Madge doesn't seem too concerned, even when Norman disappears at night for long walks on the beach, a habit newly-acquired.

When I tell Aramis, he nearly falls off the boat laughing.

'She is a street girl from the harbour, by the Navy base.'

'A prostitute?'

'Yes. She's been on the streets for three years already.'

'What's she doing out here?'

'Her family is from Skiathos, so the police chase the girls off the street for the Nato, she come back here for a few months.'

How to tell Norman? He thinks he's in love with a simple, sweet country girl, not a teenaged tart. I decide this is one for Pincher. He loves a challenge. Maria leaves for Skiathos by the next available transport, a lobster boat. Pincher pays her off well and she looks well pleased with her chubby, corrupt, little self. Her round bottom rolls cheekily as she walks down to her lobster boat, rich enough to be able to wait until the police stop cracking down on tarts near Athens, even if they take their time about it.

'What happened, Norman?'

'Well, Mr Dobermann told me the whole sad story. Her mother died, and she had to go back to her island to look after her. Wonderful girl that.'

'Aren't you going to see her again?'

'No. Mr Dobermann says that she will be in mourning for a year at least, not able to talk to any men. You know, Penny, I don't want to be crude, but I couldn't wait that long to get a bit of the you-know-what again.'

As he says it, he runs his hand over my bottom.

'Welcome back to the land of the living, Norman.'

So we leave with a full complement. The flight to the States is uneventful, even a little sad. It's been the most wonderful few months for everybody. Jens and his two girls invite us all to come to his house in the Virgin Islands, the Perlmutters want me to come and see my part of the horse run his first race – invitations fly. By the time we land at Albuquerque, we are in a thoroughly miserable state. Hiram is there to greet us, along with Jim, but no sign at all of Rick.

Hiram reads my mind.

'Rick is still a bit sore with you, but I think he'll come round, honey. He's a mite touchy about that sort of thing, but I explained to him that you European girls were brought up in a more liberal tradition, so to speak. Yup, I think he'll come round in the end.'

'I do hope so, Mr Firefly, because I have missed him terribly.'

'Good girl, now you get the guests out to the Ranch for the last party, and then you and Kate are going to have a good vacation. I've released Jim and Rick from duties for a week.'

The long convoy of Cadillacs heads out for the Firefly Ranch. All this sage brush and wide, empty landscape makes me think of Rick more than ever. But he's not there at our farewell party. Jim and Kate have made it up, so I feel doubly left out. All the guests are bedded down, Kate is nowhere to be seen, and I creep to my silent, lonely bed, feeling like the end of the world. Everyone else has got somebody, everyone else is so happy, and here I am, Penny Sutton, grass widow, unloved, unwanted, on the shelf.

I peel off my trousers, carefully fold my silk shirt, take off my bra, and am standing only in my pants, when there's a knock at the window.

'Who is it?'

'It's the Lone Ranger.'

'Oh Rick, Rick.'

'Can I come in?'

'You know us European girls, very liberal, of course you can.'

'Honey, I've missed you so much. I am sorry for my childish behaviour.'

'Rick, forgive me, too, you know how it is, I can't pretend. But I've been thinking about you so much, you and your white rhino, and the pool up in the hills.'

'Jesus, you look even more beautiful that ever. I love a suntan. Come here, let me kiss you. And again.'

'Hello, what's this? You seem to have brought your rhino's horn with you.'

'That's not a rhino horn, honey, here just take a look.'

'You've been doing exercises.'

'Trouble is, I haven't been doing any.'

'Last one into bed is a monkey's uncle.'

'That's not fair, you've got no clothes on.'

'Well, you'll have to hurry, won't you.'

'Open the curtains, let's have the moonlight. I'm embarrassed.'

'A big boy like you shy, come now. Oh, Rick, that feels so good.'

'And this?'

'Fantastic. Oh yes, yes wonderful.'

'You are sensational. I was beginning to forget. Oh Jesus, baby, I want you.'

'Come on, Rick, come on, darling. Yes, that's it. Do it to me, oh yes, do it to me. Oh darling.'

'You've got that funny walk again,' says Kate in the morning.

'I don't care if I waddle like a duck.'

'How is your cowboy?'

'Out of this world, how's yours?'

'Penny, don't laugh, but I think I could get quite fond of him.'

I do laugh, because I know that Kate is smitten. We both have the ability to distinguish between casual and serious affairs. I know that Kate is really hooked this time, despite having been with her water-skiing virtuoso only two nights ago. He was just something to pass the time.

All the guests leave in the course of the morning; I am fond of all of them, or almost all. Big Chuck comes out to pick up Bridget, who says,

'Goodbye, Mr Dobermann, see you at the terminal Monday.'

Jens and the two girls all kiss me fondly, Norman and Madge head for the airport, everyone goes in dribs and drabs, till just Kate, me, Rick, Jim and the family are left.

Hiram is very enthusiastic about the whole venture. It's been a success on every count. Pincher has given us a particularly good report not for entirely unselfish reasons, I am sure but still, Hiram wants us to help plan and operate the next trip. But we don't need to start thinking about it for more than a week.

'These boys are going to take you to a very special little cabin I've built up in the mountains near Taos, so's you can relax and do what you like, and I look forward to seeing you again in a week, wound right down and full of great ideas to make the next trip even better. Now, boys, off you go and fill the plane up with gas, get her checked over, and you can leave this afternoon.'

How he loves to be generous. Of course, with Hiram you have to earn it, but once he likes you nothing is too good. He takes me aside.

'I told you he would come round. Kinda old-fashioned we are out here in the west. Man's gotta change though. Rick, now he's a boy with a lot going for him.'

At this moment, their biplane comes low over the roof of the ranch-house.

'There they go now.'

Rick waggles the wings, and we can actually see Jim waving. We watch them go off into the distance. Suddenly there's an explosion.

'Oh my Christ,' says Hiram. 'Quick, get the ambulance and the fire-engine.'

A pall of smoke rises from the hills and a huge mushroom of flame.

Nobody can explain what happened. One moment they were flying in the clear sky, the next the plane had blown up. The Firefly family all pressed us to stay, but after the funeral, Kate and I took the first plane to London.